Time and Time Again

The Survivor

Douglas E. Wiese

Time and Time Again
The Survivor

Library of Congress Control Number: 2023905253
ISBN-13: Paperback: 978-1-64749-877-1
ePub: 978-1-64749-878-8

Printed in the United States of America

GoToPublish LLC
1-888-337-1724
www.gotopublish.com
info@gotopublish.com

CONTENTS

CHAPTER ONE

I realize full well that the human mind is a very powerful machine and that it is a medical or scientific fact that we only activate a very small portion of the real capacity that we actually have.

My own mind, I have always believed, was active enough. In some things I have excelled and in some things I have lacked. If I had been the only survivor in the incident I might have been inclined to believe that my mind had somehow caused it all, but the fact is there had been five discovered survivors at least and the possibility of several more. At least this is what I have learned in later years.

I don't recall the actual date except that it was the summer of 1989 in the month of July, sometime after the Fourth. At that time I was working at a little cut stock mill where the wages weren't the best. Why I had to be working at a place like this was beyond me. I was fifty years old and had five years of vocational and educational training past my high school years. Besides that the Army had put me through medical school so I should have been a doctor.

I worked right outside summer and winter so maybe it was the summer sun that had been beating down on my head that had caused me to feel so depressed about the way things were in the world. To me it seemed almost as if the laws were made to protect the criminal and lawless. It seemed that the honest man stood in jeopardy if he tried to protect his own rights and would often be tried and found guilty. Everything seemed to be based on influence and money and that was something I had neither of.

The ideas of cloning people, surrogate mothers and all the scientific means of bringing about birth without natural parenthood bothered me also. Artificial and synthetic were words that I wished somehow just weren't around. I had been trained as a mechanic and had worked on everything from airplanes to diesel rigs, but the new cars that were coming out needed computers to even do a simple task like changing the oil.

The experience and training that I had seemed useless in the world I lived in due to advancement and modern technology.

My folks had moved to the town of Madras in the winter of 1946 and, although I was then only in grade school, I loved the area because it was sparsely populated and life was simple. I was now living in Bend about forty miles to the south of Madras. Bend had always been the biggest town in the Central Oregon territory, but now it was like a bustling big city. The traffic was sometimes unbelievable.

Many times as I stood working at the little mill or as I looked at one of the several dams on the rivers, or as I would examine one of the fading old roads or highways, I would wish I could turn back the time clock to less complicated years. On the road that ran past the mills there seemed to be a constant run of dump trucks and earth moving equipment going by so sometimes I would imagine them taking the material back to where it had originally come from. My wife had often said that I was too nostalgic even to the point of being paranoid about it and as I say perhaps the sun had baked my brains.

That day I remember so well, yes, even though it was more years ago than I ever imagined possible. The fact is that since the effects of that day wore off of me I have forgotten not one small detail of the events, I reveal to you, if I wish to escape into the past all I have to do is close my eyes and it is all there as vivid and clear as if time was non-existent. A benefit I suppose of being a survivor.

I had injured my back severely in the year of 1967 and as I got out of bed that morning the pain between my vertebrae was hard to cope with. I had to concentrate on the movement of my legs. The digital alarm clock had not gone off though, so I had to hurry. Although it was not yet six o'clock in the morning I had trouble getting onto the highway into town. The traffic was heavy and as if that wasn't enough, some idiot in a sports car of some kind nearly forced me off the road while passing in a no passing zone. The seven miles into town often seemed like an obstacle course to me and on that day it was no exception. My job at the mill was to stack two by six inch boards that came to me on a belt out of a little hole in the side of the building that housed the planer.

The first indication to me was a strange feeling in my chest. I couldn't describe it for I wasn't sure if it was a pressure or if it was the kind of feeling you get as a premonition of excitement. While the question rolled through my mind as to what the feeling might be, I noticed the sky began to turn to a glassy but hazy blue cast. The ash from Mount Saint Helens eruption in 1980 had caused the same kind of overcast so I was sure another one of the mountains in the Cascade Range had erupted. The cement beneath my feet began to tremble just before the flash came and engulfed everything. In fact for a time I seemed to be suspended within its eerie glow. I had always believed in a God that would someday come and reclaim the earth that he had created. So I wondered if this was the time for that event. I know only that I was still alive, at least I thought so, but it was some time before I felt any terra-firma under my feet or body. When once again I felt solidity I was in the prone position so I just laid there until the yellow glow from the flash began to dissipate. Although there seemed to be a jaundice cast for the rest of the day it soon cleared enough to see. I was lying near the office so I got up and ran back to the mill. The planer was not running. In fact there seemed to be no one around. Most of the mill was in another building so I ran in there but again I found no one. The next concern on my mind was my family at home. I had to find out if they were at the house, I had to find out if they were all right. My pickup didn't seem to want to start and when it finally did it clattered as if there was no oil in the crankcase. The 350 engine had run smooth and although the truck was old, everything worked real well, but now as I put it into gear it acted as though the clutch was badly out of adjustment. As I got the truck rolling the front end began to shimmy. The power of a strong engine was gone, but I was able to keep it moving.

To my amazement the traffic lights were all non-operative nor did they need to be because I was the only one around. There were cars that seemed to have run off the road, but I never saw anyone anywhere along the road.

Perhaps it was the eerie yellow glow on everything, or just the shock of the event that I didn't understand, but as I drove the route that had been so familiar to me, questions began to plague my mind. How long had I been suspended in the yellow glow? I began to wonder if time itself had stood still somehow. Another thought that came to mind was maybe I had just been transported to another dimension where I could only see objects and not people. I looked to see the mountains that had seemed so close, but still the yellow haze or glow limited vision to about one half mile. The thought of a nuclear attack seemed likely, but where was everyone? I mean if everyone else had been invited to some flashy party, why wasn't I?

As I was to make the turn into the Deschutes River woods my brake pedal went clear to the floor and stayed there. And then later as I turned up the bumpy road to my place the back of my pickup sagged down and it ground to a halt. Steam was rolling out from under the hood as I examined the damage in the back. The axle, housing and all had just broken off and the wheel was laying off at the side of the road. My own attitude was an amazement to me. The old pickup that I had depended on and cared for, now had served its last task for me and I turned and ran down the road unconcerned.

Everything seemed to be in place at home, but again no one was there. I ran from room to room hollering and looking for my wife or daughters. In the living room I reached to turn on the television. Surely something would be on the news. As I turned the switch to "on", the set and the stand on which it sat disintegrated to become a pile of dirt and rubble on the floor. When I reached for the telephone there was the same reaction. Perhaps it was because of these two incidents coupled with my pickup falling apart that brought me, at least part way out of my shock. I had been motivated and activated by my mind but my attitude had been unaffected. As I walked back through the house though anger overtook me. I yelled my anger at a world that had taken my family and left me in an atmosphere of decay. I slammed my bedroom door and stamped my foot to the floor and the door with its casing slid down the hallway rotting away as it went. One of the beams from the open beam ceiling of the bedroom gave way leaving a gaping hole to reveal the yellow glow of the sky above. I slowly and carefully walked out of the house. Near the door was the juniper wood clock that had stopped at 9:42. How long ago that had been, I had no idea. The clock had stopped as though time itself no longer existed.

I began to walk through the yard looking at the things that had meant a lot to me. Destructible items they were, but in a world of prestige and wealth. I was sure now they had been greatly misjudged. My bus that I had converted to a motorhome stood there, its tires flat and in the yellow glow of a changing world it had become of no value at all.

Maybe this was all a dream that I would soon awaken from and maybe it was to teach me a stronger meaning of real value. I had been quite disgusted by a man who, by placing more value on his airplanes than he did his family he caused his divorce. Now, here I stood in a world I did not understand, looking at my bus, my classic Chevy and my house, knowing somehow, they were no longer mine and perhaps never were.

To tell the honest truth I don't recall being sleepy or tired at all, but with my mind racing thought against thought, I laid down under one of the pine trees that stood as though nothing had happened. As my head touched the ground I noticed a rumble that seemed to be coming from below the surface of the ground. The ground also had a vibration that made it feel as though I was sitting in one of those massaging easy chairs. I can only view the next events as those of a dream during fitful sleep for that is what it most assuredly seemed to me. In my dream I had somehow gotten to some place overseas like maybe England or Germany and there had met a woman who like myself was in a confusing world of dream. We began to have children until the area where we were was highly populated. In the dream world I suppose anything is possible and in my dream world this lasted five hundred years and then the woman disappeared. In normal thinking I surely wouldn't have blamed her if it had only been twenty years. Shortly thereafter the woman disappears though, and I find myself pushing my way through desert and jungle trying to find my way home. Until new light was shared with me of the happenings of that day, I just interpreted the dream as those of a stressful man looking for the family he once had.

Morning dawned bright and clear. Never had I seen the sky so blue nor the trees so green. The puffy white clouds high in the sky almost seemed to be a fluorescent white. The only sounds I heard were the chirping of birds in the trees and the slight whisper of a gentle breeze rustling the pine needles on the branches above my head. I once again closed my eyes, having not really noticed much more of my environment until the gentle whinny of a horse brought me to awakened reality. At the edge of the little clearing was the sturdy buckskin riding horse and two black pack horses. Each horse was tied to a tree with a long leather strap. The packs and saddle were at my head and I was laying in my bed roll which was made up of tanned and softened hides. At my sides near the rocks was the coals and ash of a burnt out campfire. The lava flow identified the place as just across the road from my home, but as I looked there wasn't any road and no houses to be seen. I had not taken off my moccasin type leather boots so I just got up and walked toward the place where I figured my house had been. There were no signs of man ever having been there before. Behind my house on the back side of my property there had been a cinder pit. Yet as I could tell, where the pit had once been was a rather high knoll. I climbed the hill and on top I climbed a tree for a better view, but as far as my vision took me there was no sign of man's changes. To the northeast I saw Pilot Butte, but again I didn't see any road on its side as there had been. I looked to the south and saw Lava Butte not far away, but again I didn't see any road on its side. Toward the city of Bend I saw no smoke stacks from the big mills and no buildings. On the distant hills there were no clear places where loggers had cut down all the trees. As I walked back through the area that I had once claimed as my own, I realized that all that could claim as my own was in the campsite not far away. My heart felt light and I began to laugh, and laugh I did, until it seemed my sides would split. A breeze ruffled my beard. Yes, I had a long beard and as I put my hand under it to pull it into vision I found it to be as white as the puffy clouds overhead. I pulled a wisp of hair from my head into view and it too was snowy white. Somehow much time had passed that I had not been aware of. Which way had it passed though? It was plainly obvious that more had passed than just a night's sleep under a pine tree. I was perhaps like Rip Van Winkle in the nursery rhyme, but my own outfit was that of an early frontiersman. Was this the year of two-thousand something or had I somehow been rushed backwards in some kind of time capsule? Whichever way it might be I wasn't sure, but I sure liked what I was seeing and must see more of this beautiful land unspoiled by man and machine.

The tracks had come along the lava flow and from the south and I was tempted to see how far I could follow them to see where I had been, but my greater desire was to see the canyons and the cove that I had loved. I guess no one place on this earth had meant to me what that place had meant. In sixty-one, though they had built a dam on the river to bury it under three-hundred feet of water. If now the earth was as never touched by man, I must see the cove again.

It was easy to judge the direction of my travel with the snowy peaks of the Cascade Range on my left side. The time of the year seemed to be early spring because the air was yet crisp and the mountains were heavy with snow. New life flourished, with little flowers and buds blossoming forth. Animals were plentiful. How many deer I saw, I lost count of. It seemed an injustice to me how that every hunting season everyone had been out to get the big buck until there just weren't enough around to service all the does. Now as I rode through the woods the big bucks were plentiful now, a beauty to behold, they did not seem to be afraid of the sight of me.

So many things I began to notice that were so different than before. Some things that had been just taken for granted. As I rode through the woods I saw stumps, but they were winter fall stumps that were not flat. Perhaps there would be those that beavers gnawed down, but it was just such things as this that created in me a feeling of complete peace and fulfillment. My mind no longer needed to be filled with concerns of nuclear waste and destruction. I had become part of a brand new world and I would make the most of it. I would cherish each moment while it lasted.

With no roads or trails, travel was slow, yet the only rush I felt was my own strong desire to see more of the land before me. It was mid-afternoon when I came to the river. For a while I just sat on my horse looking at how it made an almost semi-circle before flowing in a westerly direction. I was in a clearing where sagebrush had taken control. This particular land looked so familiar to me and it made me realize even more fully I was now looking at this area as if it had never been touched or hampered with, but it sure was in that very area now off to my right some distance, that I had stood hour after hour stacking boards at the little mill.

Once again questions flooded my mind. How long ago had it actually been since that day? My own body, and I was positive it was the same one as before, had taken some mighty changes. Although I was sure it was corporeal. I wasn't wearing glasses, but my vision was as keen as I had ever imagined it could be. I had gotten rather hard of hearing, but even as I sat there on my horse I could hear a bird preening its feathers and twittering on a tree branch some fifty feet away. The pain in my back was gone and I felt young and energetic, yet my hair was as white as if I were a hundred years old.

The earth surface itself seemed impossible, for it had regressed to originality without the slightest clue of a lost society. Or at least this part of it.

I had taken the horses down to the river's bank and was a short distance away when they began to act rather uneasy. I immediately looked to the rock ledge above them and saw the big cougar crouching and ready to pounce. Like lightning my hand went for the knife at my side and with a strength that I hadn't felt since I was a teenage kid, the knife left my hand. My aim and speed was deadly as the knife sank deep into the cat's neck slicing his jugular vein and vital nerves. The big cat had just started his leap when the knife hit so he fell short of his target.

The incident triggered another question in my mind. I had quite a store of knowledge of things that would do me no good now, but somehow this knowledge had been transferred to fit the situation. Over the next few years I would be quite amazed at the things I would do almost as by instinct, yet my knowledge of the past had not left me and through the years some of it I would take advantage of also.

I would also take full advantage of the big cat and that would take time so I figure I'd set up camp where I was. I had a lean-to type shelter that I set up on poles that I had taken from the trees along the river. There seemed to be plenty of good grass around so I figured the horses wouldn't wander far, besides they seemed to come well at my whistle.

As I unsaddled my riding horse something caught my eye that I hadn't noticed that morning. The saddle seemed to be rather new (Although I placed it as a real old Spanish style) but, behind the cantle was an inscription. On one line it said, "Vaya con dios mi Amigo." And on the second line beneath "Mi Amigo" it said, "Mi Amore." Something rang a bell within my mind and I could almost see loving, but tearful faces bidding me farewell. Mexico was a long ways away by horseback, but at that point I was tempted to go to Mexico and try to find those tearful faces wherever they might be.

The big cat's hide was soon on a stretch between four poles. Amongst my utensils I had a big pot in which I put water to boiling. I soon found a hemlock tree that I stripped the bark from, to boil in the water to create the solution I would use to tan the hide.

I also took the intestine of the cat and cut it into long fine strips to clean and cure and weave into a fine twine. To some it might seem gross but the meat from the cat was quite tasty, and my supply of jerky was replenished.

When I finally left that camp I had spent almost 7 days there, but I had new head gear that looked like the cougar's head was an extension of mine. I had a good supply of strong twine with which I could sew new clothing and a good strong hide with which I could make them out of. All in all much of the big cat traveled with me as I followed the river on northward.

Once again I came to a place where the river turned westward and I knew that this river bend was the very place that had given a bustling community its name in a different era and time. If a person was traveling north this was the last place he would see the Deschutes River for many miles. The old timers in the other time wouldn't see water again until they crossed the Crooked River at a place called Trail Crossing. By this time I was sure those roads were no longer there so I had the choice of following the river and fighting the canyons, or going to the O'Neil area and crossing there. In the other time with its fast pace, it would have only been a thirty minute ride, but now I knew it could take me a day or even more.

Some of the people of the other time I surely missed and if it hadn't been for such things as the inscriptions on my saddle, I would have wondered if I was the only human in a big world in a new time.

As I left the river and the tall pine trees behind, the land stretched out before me. The juniper trees now took over in a drier area with sage brush and rock outcroppings to find a trail around. Far ahead I could see the Smith Rock, Grey Butte and Grizzly Mountain and used them as my guide. Smaller knolls looked so familiar and yet so different.

Deer were still plentiful and jackrabbits and cottontails darted from bush to bush disappearing into their holes in the ground. Even though the juniper trees were plentiful they were shorter than the pine trees. On some high places I could see greater distances. Maybe it was because the sky was so clear and blue, but as I looked at the Cascade Range to the west and to Grey Butte and Grizzly to the north, they seemed quite a bit higher than they had been in the other time. Broken top, of the range, seemed to be as high as Jefferson had been and Jefferson peak seemed to reach into space itself.

There had been no sign of human life where the city of Bend once stood along the river and in like manner there were only juniper and sagebrush where the busy and noisy town of Redmond had been. As near as I could tell I was passing through the area about where the irrigation canal had run.

Once again the thought of time ran through my mind. Had I really lived in a modernistic world with its high technology and population explosion problems, or had this been a prophetic vision of some kind? No, I could remember my childhood back to when I was not yet two years old. Again, the only feasible conclusion I could come up with was that the time clock of space and eternity had been turned back somehow. Something had taken place on the day of the yellow glow that was far more immense than my finite mind was capable of dealing with at this present time,

If I crossed the Crooked River in the O'Neil area then my best route would be to go up the valley of Lone Pine on the backside of Grey Butte. From high points I could see up that valley, and at first I didn't see any sign of human life there either. At the top of the next knoll where I could see up the valley, it became evident to me that there was some kind of activity going on about an equal distance from the river as myself. After a little while of observation I could tell it was a slow moving dust cloud moving toward the river. By my calculation, whatever it might be, it would reach the river a short time after I did. It could be a large herd of deer or antelope coming from Grizzly Mountain to the waters of the river, but at that distance I couldn't tell.

Before going on down to the river I took a stance within a little grove of trees where my vision would not be impaired. My wait wasn't long for soon the tribe of Indians came over the hill on the opposite side of the river. They definitely were not a war party for the women and children were there. Anyway they didn't appear to be fierce or savage to me. I decided to make myself seen while they were at the distance they were. Then if I needed to take an evasive action of some kind, I could to my advantage.

I rode into plain sight on the little knoll and sat there watching them come for some time before I was noticed. I must not have posed an immediate threat to them for when they stopped, the children still played about while the women and others looked on as with great curiosity. Soon three men rode to the river's edge and stopped there, so I did the same. The three men seemed young and I was sure the one in the middle was the chief. There was nothing said for a while as we sat there on our horses on opposite banks of the river. I finally, slowly walked my horse onto the river holding my right flat palm up to them. They gave me room but formed a semicircle around me. They had their weapons as I had mine, but there was no gesture toward them. I did take off my cougar head hat and put it on the saddle horn in front of me though. They soon began to talk amongst themselves and an amazement to me began to occur. Very quickly I picked up a word they were saying and as if that word was the key to their language I began to be able to put it together enough to understand them, or at least the idea of what they were discussing.

They had determined that I was indeed a man and not some kind of animal. I rode a horse like them. I was dominant over animals and wore their hides as my covering just as the Indians did. My skin was lighter than theirs though and I had a lot of hair on my face.

While they were discussing I was aware of every movement around me. Very soon I noticed some of the rest of the tribe creeping in for a closer look. It was obvious that they had never seen a white man before.

After a while I slowly got down off my horse and walked back to my pack where I had some Mexican type jewelry and trinkets. Again very slowly I walked up away from the river to where I saw a little girl I judged to be about ten years old. I didn't see any fear on her face as she stood there so still. So I gently slipped a necklace over her head and walked back to where the chief was. Only then did it occur to me that my gesture might appear as though I was asking for the little girl and I began to laugh. When I did the rest of them also began to laugh. I handed the rest of the trinkets to one of the young braves and pointed to some of the other children. He quite well understood for he soon ran off to deliver the goods to the other delighted children.

It was obvious that I had at least established a good standing with them and they soon moved up the river a ways to set up their camp and I set up where I had crossed.

Fishing had never been much good on this part of the Crooked River before, but as I stood on the bank looking into the clear water I saw a number of good sized fish swimming there, so with careful aim and a strong thrust I soon had a brown trout wiggling on the end of my spear.

As I feasted on my catch and took care of the other duties of my camp I was fully aware of eyes that peered at me from behind bushes and trees along the river. Soon a big full moon came up over the ridge making the night time as bright as day and I fell asleep with a feeling of total peace and serenity.

I became aware of the day far later than I had hoped to. A cloud bank was rolling over the Cascade Range and the wind that was blowing had dropped the temperature to an almost uncomfortable level.

Quite to my astonishment I found two Indian woven blankets draped over my packs. I quickly topped the ridge to where I could see the river, to the south, until it went around the bend and was hidden by the canyon walls. There, also ready to go around the bend was a cloud of dust caused by many feet. I was sure I would see them again, but as I stood watching then disappear around the bend a feeling of loneliness swept over me. There was a purpose to all this and I was sure I would find it.

People are destructible items also. They appear on the surface of the earth for a short time. They try to be important and wise and like to feel needed and loved, but they soon grow old and feeble and are gone and most often soon forgotten. Many times a slight mistake in judgment and their lives are snuffed out very quickly. As I stood there that morning I began to wonder what wisdom and knowledge was all about. I had known a lot of people with a long list of college degrees attached to their names, but where were they now? What good would those degrees do if they stood with me at that moment? It seemed to me that the only wisdom or knowledge that was of any real value was that which was possessed by the one who ruled the entire universe. Man had even gotten to the place to have said, "God is dead." No situation is totally secure. Nothing indestructible. Everything is subject to change and man, huh, what a finite being to be so proud. I felt rather humbled to have been chosen for whatever the purpose of my existence was.

Although the day was to be considered rather chilly, the river soon became the place for me to bathe and frolic in and it was invigorating to say the least. I knew that at this time of the year the river's water would be chilled by melting snow. When I came out of the river, I knew I was clean and I stood facing the glowing sun and cried to the only one that might be able to hear me. My expression as I stood there naked and open in his sight, was that as I hid nothing from him that he might hide nothing from me, and as I had done what I could to cleanse my body, that he might do what he could to cleanse my soul. I desired and ask that I would do nothing to bring destruction or waste upon the land. To my knowledge it had once been cleansed by flood. Once again it had been cleansed by a force I could not explain, but as for me I would do my best to retain the natural beauty I saw.

By the time my ritual was over the sun was more than half over the sky. I would set up my lean-to, in case of rain and I would spend another night at this spot by the river.

Morning came early for me as far as I could tell. The sky was beginning to turn light, but the rain was falling quite heavy. Fog and clouds obscured the tops of the nearby buttes and wisps of fog hung along their sides to give them a mystic appearance.

I was soon packed and was heading up the Lone Pine Valley. I remembered, in the other time, of driving truck for a large ranch in this valley, but there certainly wasn't any ranch here now. The valley seemed fertile enough and a little spring and mountain fed stream ran through it. The valley ended at the foot of Grizzly Mountain. I followed the base of Grey Butte around until I was facing a westerly direction then I began looking for the other buttes along this cluster. Whereas Mount Jefferson was hidden from view by the clouds I would use Haystack and Juniper Buttes as my guides to lead me to the canyons and the cove.

By early afternoon the clouds had begun to lift and the rain had stopped. I could see across the canyons to the foothills of the Cascade Range. Hogback Ridge was so clear in my view that it seemed I could reach out and touch it. I could now see the plateau that the north end lay above where the Crooked River and Deschutes River came together and was the place called the cove. As I had usually let the horses just walk along picking their way I now put them into a fast trot. My heartbeat seemed to increase the closer I got.

There was a little side spur to the main canyon that would give me access without having to scale a rim rock. And I came to it as if a trail had led me there. The spur led me down onto a wide flat part of the canyon, but in the middle of this was where it dropped very steeply to the river. In some places the rock walls were as much as two hundred feet high. I came to a very narrow place where the rock cliffs gave way to a steep sloped hillside, in the other time this had been the place they had blasted out to put a road through to reach the bottom.

This place in the canyon had been so familiar to me in the other time and until they had put the dam in and flooded this particular area, it had been like a refuge to me. Now as I stood at the edge of the canyon I could see the river far below, the area that had been an orchard, across the river to the place that had been a beautiful park. I looked through the saddle between the peninsula and the plateau and could see the other canyon. The Deschutes River was in that canyon and at the north end of the plateau it would merge with the Crooked River. As I stood there under a darkening sky everything seemed to be in the right perspective, all right but at somewhat larger dimensions. Mount Jefferson loomed high in the twilight sky around it.

I decided to set my camp back a ways on the ledge and wait until morning to descend into the canyon, but through the night the view of the canyon and the mountains never left my mind.

Many times, when I had started to feel boastful about my own self and accomplishments I had come to this place where the high vertical cliffs had made me feel as insignificant and small as the ants crawling around at my feet. If there actually was (and I most assuredly believed there was) a supreme being to control all this world then man's boastfulness must surely seem like foolishness to such a one.

Once again questions, concerning events between the other time and the current time, began to invade my mind. Had the earth somehow stretched itself thus freeing itself of man's wrinkles or had the members of the mammal and animal kingdom shrunk to some degree? I or the Indians didn't seem to be out of perspective with the trees and shrubbery of the earth. The distance that I had traveled even seemed to be about right, but yet all the hills had seemed to be higher which made the valleys seem deeper. Perhaps it was the clearness of the sky without pollutants.

So many things approached me, day by day, that I didn't understand, yet still I wasn't sure I needed to understand it all. I seemed to be well equipped for the environment I faced. Maybe someday I would understand it all and maybe that would be the day I would wish I could turn back the time clock to this time. Lest I forget the slightest detail I would live this time to the fullest and claim each moment as sacred and my very own.

The day dawned bright and refreshed from the previous day's rain and except for a few puffy clouds in the sky it was otherwise clear.

I had decided I would carve a trail into the canyon. The thought had at first bothered me for it would mean that the land would receive a mar of mankind at the hand of myself. Of course I had decided to set up a permanent camp by the river. In my pack I had a variety of seeds to plant so I would till the soil and perhaps build a rock house for a dwelling.

Where I had crossed the river at O'Neil it had been rather calm, the water was deep being it was the springtime of the year, but here at the cove the river was a raging torrent. In a relatively short distance the river had dropped elevation a great deal. As I stood now on the river bank listening to it roar over the rocks, a strong emotion came over me. I had finally reached home. I would travel the countryside and enjoy its beauty, but here in the canyon with its high rock walls I would be sheltered and to this place I would somehow always return.

CHAPTER TWO

I had diverted the water from the spring that was on the hillside so that it ran right past my rock cabin and went on to water the soil I had tilled. Little green sprouts were coming up and I was sure there would soon be others. This bottom land of the canyon was very fertile. I had worked hard and the fruits of my labor were showing nicely.

A movement high upon the canyon rim caught my eye. There were a number of horses and riders there that seemed to be observing my activities. I wondered if they were the same Indians that I had met at O'Neil. I gave a shrill whistle and my horse soon came to my side. I would ride to the top of the canyon and show myself sociable. There had been no hostile action before so I saw no reason to have fear at this appearing. I had had a slight loneliness at times for the presence of other human beings and these were the only humans I had seen since my awakening.

As I rode up the trail the Indians moved along the rim to stay above me. As I rode up the small spur canyon I could see them more plainly. There didn't seem to be any women with them this time, but rather they seemed to be a hunting party. Why they were particularly interested in me at this time I wasn't sure.

When I topped the canyon the Indians kept their distance and I didn't advance any further either. It was the same chief I had met at O'Neil and I recognized several of the other young braves. The main figure with them this time was their shaman who spoke with the chief and two braves in whispered tones. Although I couldn't quite hear words

I was aware that they were showing me to the shaman for him to figure me out. Soon the shaman came alone to ride around me shaking his rattles and chanting all the while.

I wasn't wearing a shirt for the summer sun was warm and my white hair and beard were flowing in the breeze. I had thought that I would do my own dance and ritual after the shaman was through but as soon as he went back to the rest they turned and rode away. I watched them until they rode out of sight.

If only there was some way that I could get an overall view of the land and the main camp of the Indians, I could better understand their movements and thus contact them whenever I desired. It was obvious to me that I needed to impress them somehow to the positive.

My days of aviation, in the other time, came to my mind and although I wouldn't be able to construct an airplane, I might be able to build a hang glider to ride the thermals across the land. The thought began to intrigue me to a great extent. In the other time there had been a program on television called "Fantasy Island" where a magical fellow caused all kinds of people's dreams to come true. Many times it turned out to be to their displeasure. What a thought to cross my mind as though I really was in some fantasy world. Well, I could tell anyone that whoever it might be that created this scenario, they had surely gone all out, and I enjoyed it immensely.

It seemed funny how things would suddenly cross my mind like that, but soon I was riding back down into the canyon figuring it out in my head how I would accomplish the feat of building my flying contraption. The first thing would be to get a material that would be light enough to cover the thing with. Most of the leather hides I used would be far too heavy for such a craft.

Rattlesnakes had been plentiful in the canyon and many times they had tried to use my little rock shelter as a cool refuge in the heat of the day. Of course it had always been my attitude to make sure that they remained permanently cool. In return they had been nice to me by giving me a tender meaty meal. Their skin had also given me the material I would use to make my air machine.

Several weeks were employed for time while I worked on the glider. The spars for the frameworks had to be light yet sturdy and durable. Pieces for the right of center had to be identical to those that were left of center. The sling in which I would ride had to be placed at an exact center of gravity where I could control the vertical and longitudinal axis. I would control movement by shifting my own weight back and forth and to each side. Before I covered my craft I took the skins and suspended it between four poles so that it was stretched tight about two feet above the ground. I then jumped onto it several times to test its elasticity and strength.

The day of testing finally came and I took my contraption to the top of the canyon where a good breeze seems to continually blow. Facing into the wind I began to run down a little bit of an incline that was fairly free of sagebrush. The bunchgrass was high, but then it was everywhere. I soon felt the wind begin to billow within the hollows of the glider and felt my feet begin to get light on the ground. I finally pulled my weight forward and began to soar just a few feet above the ground, I pulled my weight to the side and began a gentle bank toward the shallow part of the canyon. When I came to the rim a breeze washing up over the side seemed to momentarily stop me in midair. I soon pulled my weight forward as if to swoop down into the canyon but the breeze seemed to be strong enough to carry me aloft and I began to gain altitude. I wasn't sure as yet that I wanted to trust the glider to great altitudes, but I began to circle around the thermal that I had caught and was soon about a hundred feet above the ground level at the top of the canyon. I started a wide circle over the canyon and soon saw my little rock dwelling and my horses far below.

Up until this point I hadn't really noticed my breathing or heart beat because all my concentration was on the craft up which I hung my life. I soon came to realize, though, that my heart was beating out a super-fast rhythm of excitement. The implications of the incident began to flood my mind as if by a tidal wave. At least for the time that I had found myself in, I was probably the first human to conquer air.

There only seemed to be a slight balance problem with the glider as I had to hold a slight forward pressure on it. To alleviate that I decided to sew my cougar head hat into the crevice where the front two spars began to bow to an angle toward the back. The weight and drag that it would cost I figured would be sufficient. When I had finished fastening the head, I stood back away to examine my handy work. The glider set on the control handles so the main surface was suspended a little ways off the ground. With the cougar head and the snake skin covering, it looked to be some kind of interpretation about the different multi-headed beasts mentioned in the last book of the Bible. I must admit I had had my ideas too, but now all I could really interpret was how that one Biblical preacher had said that we look through "a glass darkly," or in other words a smoky window that impaired our vision of future things. I thought of how true that seemed to me now in this time and about the time wasted in boastful arguments of what the future held. Where were those boastful people now?

The whole of the next day was spent riding the thermals that rose from the canyons and the wind shears from the various hills that dotted the countryside. The land stretched before me in a seemingly endless beauty. On the ground there were many dust devils which created a sky full of up and down drafts. Thunderheads were forming so the sky would have been rough for one of the regular airplanes from the other time, but as for my craft I was able to take full advantage of the situation. Several times I gained altitudes to where only the most prominent terrain features were detectable. I was able to glide great distances and cover a lot of ground. By evening the sky had gotten dark and foreboding and I knew a thunderstorm was coming in quick. I had been looking over the Trout Creek area and was near the Willowdale Valley and knew I would have to put down there.

I set up my craft on some poles a distance from the creek so that it would act as a lean-to. I also set up a snare and caught a cottontail rabbit that was scurrying for shelter in the face of the storm. The rabbit had just completed his tasty service to me when the storm hit with all its wild loud fury.

The storm seemed to cover a vast area for everywhere I looked the sky was dark with clouds. The clouds swirled in war-like fury, turning a near green at times. The sky was yet light on the horizon to the south, which gave the area an awesome atmosphere. Water and hail soon began to pour from the sky in such a manner as to leave torrents running through each little ravine.

As I sat under my shelter my mind couldn't help but envision the scenes of the day. I had followed the Crooked River clear to the Prineville area. There I had caught a thermal near Grizzly Mountain that had taken me to great heights. I had then followed Willow Creek through the Madras area and down the canyon to the Deschutes River. Much of the area near where the town of Warm Springs had been was beneath my eye as I soared overhead. From there I had found Trout Creek and had come to the area where I now sat watching the storm.

I drifted off to sleep and woke sometime during the night. A bright moon revealed a cloudless sky and the roar of a storm swollen torrent lapped a few yards from my shelter. If I had known this country in the other time, then I was aware of what violence the sudden thunderstorm would bring. I had seen water come through this same valley with such force and volume as if the mighty Deschutes had changed its course.

The following day was very calm and clear and I knew there would be no sailing the thermals. Although I carried my glider to the top of a nearby hill only to drift back down into the valley again. I only had my knife with me and the clothes I wore, but for me that was enough and I ended up staying and exploring the valley for a total of five days.

I would spend many days soaring over the land and feeling free. I would watch the clouds over the Cascade Range and knew the very times I could play the currents that came from the valley beyond. I was also aware of the wind shear that could have drawn me into the side of the mountains to have dashed me to bits.

I followed Indian trails, animal herds and canyons. A couple of times I crossed the mountains to see the valley beyond with its endless stand of timber. Nowhere did I see roads or buildings or destruction of the terrain. Many times I would stay a while in some place that especially intrigued me.

I used the land as I needed and it nourished me well, but I paid no taxes or rent. I had no automobile or fancy houses and yet in my own right I was a multi-millionaire. I traveled great distances and saw the country in its natural beauty.

The glider had opened the ability to cover much of the land and in a sense it gave me dominion.

Two particular incidents happened that helped me impress the Indians to my favor. These incidents in themselves gave me a perspective of an unspoiled or hampered-with world that I never would have seen in the other time.

There had been much concern about the old and aging as far as human life was concerned and it was a constant question as to what to do with the elderly, but in the animal kingdom there didn't seem to be that particular problem. With the sport of killing abounding many of the animals and different species of the bird kingdom had become known as endangered species because so many had been killed. Of course the environmentalists tried, by scientific means, to keep a natural balance, but to me that didn't ever seem adequate. I suppose there were still places where animals such as deer, bear, eagles and such could live out their lives until the fullness of time gathered them, but those places had been far and few between.

Now in this new time I had begun to see the old and aging in the animal world. Sometimes it was sad to see, but I knew this was the natural way. No one was having to program things scientifically to maintain any simulations of balance. Nature was doing the job in its own way.

I had been soaring the thermals over the area at the mountain, Three Fingered Jack, when about eighty feet below me I saw an eagle leave a rocky crag and begin to float over the valley below. Very quietly and cautiously I began to follow the eagle dropping altitude a little at a time as I did. To keep the shadow of my craft from covering the eagle I had to maneuver like a World War I flying ace in a combat dog fight. I also had to keep the skin of my glider from snapping in the breeze. Soon I was less than ten feet above him and slightly behind. Very quickly I swooped down and grabbed a handful of tail feathers. Within an instant the eagle gave a loud squawk and turned its head from side to side trying to see what had gotten him. I then noticed the milky film that covered the once bright and watchful eye of the old eagle. I glided gently away from the old eagle with my hand full of beautiful feathers, but that evening as I sat beside my little rock cabin, my heart ached for the aging eagle and the fear of the unknown that I must have placed within him. Eyes that once could have detected the movement of a mouse from great heights or another eagle up to 40 miles away now had a hard time seeing even a few feet from himself. I wondered how he existed. Eagles had their mates for life so I wondered if a loving mate took care of him. Even if that were so, he was out there still trying and I was greatly impressed.

Several months after the incident with the eagle, I was on foot in the Metolius River area. I was after a deer for my winter supply of meat, for the snow was heavy on the ground. I came to a brush thicket and found a buck caught by the horns in the tangles of the brush. An old doe stood with the buck's tail in her mouth and did not move. As I came close I found that the buck had died in his struggle to be free and the brush itself supported his weight. Upon checking the doe, I found that like the eagle she had sightless eyes and had been led by the old faithful buck. I could see the pain of uncertainty written all over the doe, but she stood hanging onto the tail waiting to be led to safety.

As gently as I could, I took my knife and cut off the tail of the buck. Holding the tail at the height that the buck would have carried it, I began to walk away and although things didn't seem quite right to her, the doe began to follow on into the unknown.

The Indians had been camped by the river about a ten mile distance so I just walked on to their camp. I had had the eagle feathers with me so I held them up before me and the doe followed behind as I walked into the Indian camp. Someone had gone to the chief even before I got there so he stood by with his braves as I came in. I walked on past him as though he was non-existent. I walked right to the old shaman's tent who had heard the commotion and came out in time for me to present my gift. The wrinkled old shaman turned to the chief and simply asked, "Why?"

The chief answered then turned to me.

"He will make shaman soup to work his magic, but he turns old and his magic will end. Many seasons ago we first saw the pale man, yet he has not aged nor has his strength weakened. He has strong magic."

The moon was bright on the snow, yet the night time had come shortly after I had left the Indian camp. As I walked the long trek home my mind heard the chief's statement over and over again. I had been at the cove about six winters now. I had worked up a calendar that I figured to be quite accurate. I had been with the Indians on numerous occasions and had learned to speak with them openly. They had still held me at arm's length, so to speak, but that night had seemed to knot the relationship between, at least the chief and I, rather close.

I had set up a rope type bridge across the Deschutes River and another across the Crooked River and as I crossed the latter the morning sun was conquering the glow of the moon on the snow.

The thought that I might have offended the old shaman bothered me greatly. My act was meant to bring about a good relationship between the Indians and myself. To a great deal it had worked and I suppose it was just the declining years of the shaman that had caused his reaction. His ego had been deflated.

Several days later I was to be with the Indians again. They had been on a hunting expedition but had had no luck. The day before I had been gliding and knew where the deer were.

We were sitting around a fire where words were few yet heartfelt emotions flowed silently, but free.

Soon I broke the silence. "If my friends want a feast in their camp tonight then they will go to the canyon where the creek flows from the Mountain of Bears to the big river." Again there was silence for a while until the chief spoke in answer.

"The pale man has many times shown friendship and strong wisdom. We will go to the place he speak of and tonight we will have a feast in our camp. Our women and children will be satisfied. We will not forget the pale man. Our camp is his camp. Our horses are his horses."

Soon the Indians were gone, but when the big bird with the cougar's head flew high above the canyon where the creek runs from the Mountain of the Bears, the Indians were far below with an abundance of meat and hides.

The summer sun was once again heating strong and hot on the rocks of the canyons. The mountains were losing their snow and again I stood observing the green plants in my garden when I saw several of the Indians appear at the place of the canyon where the trail was real narrow. Two of them came on down the trail and as they approached I recognized the chief and his son. The reason for their coming had to be urgent for never before had they come down to my own camp. The chief wasted no time in conveying the message he came to relate,

"The chief's daughter suffers great pain, perhaps soon she will go to the spirit world where she will also take my own heart. The shaman's "magic" is not strong enough. The pale man's magic is strong."

I was surely being asked to go with the chief to work my magic on his daughter.

"Where is the pain on the body of my chief's daughter?" I asked. The chief held his hand to his right side and writhed in a perfect display of his daughter's agony.

"Where is the tent of my chief's daughter?" I further inquired.

"Near the creek that flows from the Mountain of Bears. At the place where the canyon stops to begin again. I knew the place had to be the Madras area and from the chief's descriptive acting I imagined the problem to an appendix attack."

I ran into my rock shelter and got a supply of my cat gut twine and a needle made from a curved fish bone. I thought of my medical training in the other time. How long ago that had been I truly wasn't sure, but as I began to visualize the procedure of a surgery it was as though I had recently taken a refresher course.

As we rode to the top of the canyon many thoughts rushed through my mind. This could be the time of change in many things. If I was successful in bringing about a cure then I was sure that a good lasting relationship would be established which could mean many fringe benefits. If I was unsuccessful, then I was sure a complete opposite reaction would occur.

I had been storing my glider on the bench between the spur canyon and deeper parts. By observing the weather, I was sure that by using the glider I could cut the travel time at least in half and perhaps by much more.

As I strapped myself into the glider, the Indians were sure it was a great magic costume and that I had already begun my cure, but as I ran down the hill toward the drop off of the canyon wall, I'm sure their attitude changed. As I began to circle and gain altitude they stood with their eyes glued to the glider with a mixed emotion of awe, worship and wonder. They still were standing there when they were so far below me, I could barely distinguish them from the rocks along the canyon wall.

The wind at altitude was far more favorable to me than I had figured that they would be, I landed my craft on a little hill just above the creek and took note of the location of the teepee that the old shaman danced around. The teepee surely stood in the very place where my parent's little house had stood in the other time.

Tears had begun to fill my eyes and then I realized that many of the tribe had come to quizzically observe me and the glider. I realized that they were not going to bother the glider for there was too much mystery involved, and as I headed toward the teepee they began to follow me. There had been as much mystery and awe surrounding me as there was the glider.

The Indians had a concoction that they called sleeping water that put off a vapor to breathe. I wasn't sure that it would be sufficient enough for surgical procedures or not, but the shaman had given the girl enough that she was surely under the influence of it.

I had told one of the old squaws to get me some boiling water and she came to the teepee shortly after I had entered. The old shaman seemed rather disgruntled due to the fact that I was there, but he succumbed to my authority amidst displays of his disgust. I had some water that was very warm to the touch and asked the old shaman to wash very clean as far up as his elbows and not to touch anything until I was ready for him. He mumbled something about squaw's magic but began to wash. I had pulled the girls' clothing back to reveal the area of the appendix and by examining I found the hard lump of the inflamed organ beneath the skin. I had dropped my knife in the boiling water and then washed the girl and myself. One thing I was going to make sure of and that was I would fight any chance of infection that I possibly could.

I had set a couple of the braves at the door of the teepee as guards. No one was allowed in but myself and the old shaman.

So it was that with my heart beating out a hard fast rhythm and a prayer on my lips I began my first unassisted operation. I was closing the incision before I took note at all of the commotion around me. I first looked at the old shaman who now sat beside me with his face pale and eyes staring in almost unbelief. What he had seen before him he could not fathom. There was also a problem outside the teepee. The chief had evidently returned telling his people that the pale man had gone into the spirit world. The others had pointed out the glider on the hill and said that I had come from the spirit world long before the sun had reached its peak in the sky. There was much discussion about the magic dress of the pale man and the powers involved. They would not touch the costume of the pale man lest they be carried into the spirit world and never return. No wonder the pale man's magic was so strong, for he alone had the power to enter the spirit world and return as he desired.

I soon let the shaman go to his own teepee and he would have gone in silence if it had not been for the press around him. Questions bombarded the old man, questions he could not answer nor ever cared to try. "Am I the one who makes the sun to come by day and the moon by night? Am I the one who causes the seasons of the sun and seasons of the snow? Do I teach the birds to sing or the clouds to form? Do I instruct the clouds as to which one will bring rain and which one will bring shade? I only know that these things are, and I know as soon as it takes a knife wound to heal the chief's daughter will be strong again. I will now go to my teepee and a few more moons I will go to the spirit world and then I will know."

With that the shaman turned and walked on to his teepee. I knew as I watched him go that I would soon go to his tent and pay him the respect I knew he deserved. The chief came to the teepee about that time, so I explained to him the best I could, what had been wrong with his daughter and what her progress would now be. The chief just looked at his daughter for a few moments making sure she was indeed all right and then turned to look at me almost in a worship attitude. Not liking the idea, but yet not wanting to disrupt the progress that I had made. I began to talk with the chief in a way I thought he might understand.

"When my chief was very young he would look at his elders with envy at their knowledge of the bow and arrow. Now through many seasons he shoots the arrow to an accurate target without ever thinking about careful aim. Now the very young look at my chief with envy over that which they do not know. There are many things in the land to gain knowledge of. The eagle has knowledge of the air. The fish has knowledge of the water. The pale man has knowledge of many things the chief does not. The chief has knowledge of things the pale man does not. One is not greater than the other."

The chief listened intently and bowed when I was through with my little speech. And then walked out of the teepee.

I stayed with the Indians a week making sure the girl, Desert Flower, was all right. I talked with the old shaman and showed him respect, but he sat in silence. There was a pow-wow held in which I was shown honor and was christened White Cloud, by the Indians.

I learned later that two days after I left the Indian's camp the old shaman went to the spirit world where great knowledge was revealed to him. I would miss him for in his own right and time he had been a great and wisdom-filled man due honor and respect. Questions he had were now revealed, but he would not return from the spirit world like White Cloud.

CHAPTER THREE

The time that I had spent at and around the cove in this new time had surely been a pleasure to me in most ways. I had been lonely at times, but then my association with the Indians had helped that some.

My riding horse had grown old and died, but earlier I had traded my pack horses to the Indians for a young mare that was well on her way for dropping a foal. That had turned out to be a good looking stud horse and so through it all I had worked myself a nice little herd of good looking horses.

I had spent much time with my glider during especially favorable wind conditions and so all in all I kept quite busy. My life was to change to quite an extent though, and my first indication of that change was when a group of the Indians, once again, rode into my camp, they encircled the girl named Desert Flower. For some reason, although it seemed completely out of character, I knew without a shadow of doubt what the reason of the visit was. Soon we sat around in a circle except for Desert Flower who still sat on her horse looking very shy. After the usual time of silence the chief began his talk.

"Many seasons ago we met White Cloud. We did not know if he was friend or enemy. While we wondered and took counsel among ourselves, White Cloud honored our sons and daughters. White cloud showed no fear. He did not act as our enemy, but gave gifts to our children. Desert Flower even now wears the gift that White Cloud gave her many seasons ago."

I looked up at Desert Flower and sure enough the Spanish style necklace was around her neck. I was quite startled for I had not connected Desert Flower with the little girl at O'Neil.

"White Cloud has shown friendship and honor many times. Many times he has helped us and given us strength to fight our enemies. When our needs were more than wisdom of our shaman. White Cloud's wisdom and knowledge was strong. White Cloud honors our people, but his wisdom has many mysteries."

Again there was silence, yet I knew it was not my time to speak.

The chief now addresses me personally.

"Let there be no division between White cloud and my people. Many seasons from now let your children be our children, your sons be our sons.

It is the chief's desire and the desire of Desert Flower that she honor White Cloud with many sons and daughters."

It was perfectly clear that the next time the silence was broken it would be from the mouth of White Cloud.

What thoughts raced through my mind in these moments for I began to compare this incident with the way things were done in the other time? I had been married and had a family and perhaps that had been quite a miracle. You see I just didn't seem to fit into the scenario of dating, going steady and the folderol of courtship. I had just met the person I thought was right for me and had accepted it as that. I hadn't tried to put on any show or act so our going together time was very short. We were married and we raised a family and it seemed to me that we were as stable as or more so than a lot of people who had worked so hard at building a relationship.

In this case I didn't even have to go through the nerve bending agony of a proposal. The chief had done that for me. In a way that seemed rather funny to me, but I didn't laugh.

Desert Flower was a very attractive Indian girl. She wasn't the perfect body of a Hollywood movie star, but a real-to-life type. She was somewhat stocky with a well-proportioned figure. She didn't seem to be fat at all, but rather muscular. Her face had the beauty of a true princess.

"White Cloud has spent these many seasons here in this camp. His belly has not wanted for meat. He has not wanted for horses. The sky is his and has sent rain and warmth where needed. White Cloud has been busy and has been strong. White Cloud has many friends now, but sometimes when the moon lights up the night sky like day, White Cloud's heart breaks for being lonely. White Cloud was alone many seasons even before he met his friends. Now my friend has brought White Cloud a gift that makes his heart soft and warm. My sons will be your sons. My daughters will be your daughters. My horses will be your horses."

As I sat there, at that moment, looking at the old chief with long braided hair and rotting stubs for teeth, he looked beautiful to me. Inside that body, that held his wrinkled old face, was a heart as good as gold and as warm as the summer's breeze. I would challenge anyone who would doubt the presence of love within that situation, for the love I felt for those before me that day seemed to completely fill the empty place left by the loss of family and friends on the day of the yellow glow. Here there were no hidden personality flaws. None of society's etiquette rules to follow. These were real people with no pretenses or acts to play.

Desert Flower never did fit into the category of a housewife. We had the little rock shelter and later on we had a teepee that Desert Flower built. There were many chores that she took on as her personal duty and she carried them out no matter what the situation might have been. In the winter she kept the fire going. In the summer she took over my ever increasing garden. The fruits of my hunting expedition became her task. I never ask her to do anything, but her hands and her mind never quit clear up until the time she crossed the river into the spirit world.

My "trips into the spirit world," as she called it, was too far beyond the capacity of her mind to grasp. I tried to explain the principle of the glider to her, but she didn't care to understand. Her concentrated desire was to make my life as pleasant as possible and that she certainly was a professional. It was also my desire to make her life happy and I also must have been successful for she never expressed anything to the contrary.

Occasionally I would take a trip up the canyon to where a large spring ran from the side of the canyon. Deep in the crystal clear pool was a bed of pure opal. This place in the other time had been known as Opal Springs where they had blasted and encased the spring so as to pump the pure water to the surrounding communities. I had been at the spring before they encased it and as I stood there now in this time my mind was enthralled with its unhampered beauty. The spring would, from time to time, bubble up pure opal so I gathered a good share and began the task of putting together an opal necklace.

As was so often the case, the night was as clear as the day, and the moon shared its reflected light generously. With only the sound of the rushing river to break the stillness, White Cloud gently slipped the opal necklace over the head of Desert Flower. Desert Flower's smile was warm enough to melt away any loneliness that White Cloud had ever felt.

It was the summer after the first boy was born that a lone rider came into my camp. Desert Flower recognized the rider while he was still near the top of the canyon. "That is Grey Wolf. He was injured in battle with our enemy. He comes to have you work the same magic on him as you did on me."

Grey Wolf was very young and had only become a brave early that spring. I had heard that he had taken an arrow in the groin and that the shaft had broken off leaving the arrow head buried near the leg and hip joint making it difficult for him to walk.

I asked Desert Flower how long it would take to concoct some sleeping water and found out that there was a fermenting time involved. I later learned that they mixed a sulfur solution with alcohol which created an ether type substance. Grey Wolf had brought some with him, though, so there needed to be no delay.

Although there wasn't the urgency of my own reputation with the Indians involved. Still this was a human life I was dealing with and I felt it very important that I succeed.

I knew that the sciatic nerve and a main artery ran through this area and for that I needed to be very careful. The arrow head had been there for several months so I was surprised when reaching it that the vital damage was very minimal. There was some devitalized tissue and there was a chipped bone, but other than that I was sure Grey Wolf would be able to walk fine with little or no pain. The pain he must have felt while carrying the arrow head must have been severe.

Desert Flower acted as my nurse and followed my instruction with precision. Her expressions were of quite a different nature for in her mind she was trying to bring a comparison to her own experience.

Grey Wolf stayed with us until his wounds were mostly healed. Several times he gave us a demonstration of how he could walk again. He even demonstrated how he could do a rain dance. Our son had been born during a thunderstorm and Grey Wolf thought if he could dance up another storm then perhaps another baby would be born.

Our son having been born during an early spring thunderstorm, Desert Flower had immediately named him Thunder Cloud. Grey Wolf's magic was strong even if it was a little slow in action. Another son was born on a cold winter day three years later and appropriately Desert Flower named him Grey Cloud. My name in the other time had been Dean Williams, but now, in this new time, at this humble canyon dwelling, there lived the Cloud family.

I spent much time with the boys, training them as best as I could. The most important things in this time seemed to be the things of nature. There was so much to see and learn. I taught the boys how one could sit still in one place and see active life in progress from the small to the great all around them. Little bugs of all descriptions scurrying to and fro in acceptance of life and the task before them. Birds that seemed in constant motion. Bobcats that walked so softly as not to miss the slightest sound that might mean either danger or a meal. Deer whose grace and beauty brought them swiftness and agility. The supreme one who had created it all, though, had instilled in man the ability to learn something from each of these beings that would assist him in his claim to life. Within the very nature of man, was and is, the ability to rise far above the most intelligent animal, or to fall to a degrading place far below the most insignificant animal or creeping thing that ever did exist.

I did not tell my family about the other time and the way things had become, nor did I warn them that time would probably do the same again. Only once did Desert Flower question my origin and it wasn't questioned again for many long years. I cherished the times of the Cloud family and hung on to the experience as long as I could. Some knowledge I found unnecessary to share.

Thunder Cloud, from the beginning, as if by the very nature of his name, had more the nature of a bobcat. He accepted all and everything as an enemy that had to be proven. Only his own kinship was exempt and as that kinship got distant, so did his openness and trust. His keen sense made him aware of every movement about him. Nothing evaded his ear or eye. He could traverse in and out of the canyon with the swiftness of the deer and without sound.

Grey Cloud, although as agile in speed and strength, was more trusting by nature. Nothing escaped his awareness either. Yet in everything he found beauty and good. Grey Cloud's very nature was to search out the positive value of every being even though it might be difficult to find.

The two sons of White Cloud were inseparable even though their personalities were so different, and so it was the older they got, the more they were drawn to their maternal heritage. Their love for White Cloud was often expressed in word and deed and never was their leaving of a rebellious nature. White Cloud had no enemies for he would not allow it to be so. Desert Flower's people had their enemies and it had been so since their first existence. Thunder Cloud felt it to be his obligation to fight for and with his mother's people and fight he did. So many were his victories that he became war chief for the tribe.

Often was the case that one or two wounded would be brought to White Cloud after a battle with the enemy from the south. White Cloud's magic was very strong and the Indians were amazed at the differences in White Cloud's magic and the magic of their own shaman.

An uncle of Grey Wolf's was the new shaman. His name was Broken Horse, but he would have little to do with White Cloud. It wasn't as though there was any animosity between Broken Horse and White Cloud. It was just that White Cloud's ways were new and different from the way of the Indian and Broken Horse preferred the old way with no changes. Grey Cloud and Thunder Cloud were the same when it came to the old Indian ways. Although they had grown up with White Cloud, still there was a dividing point which the Indian would not cross. This included the sons of White Cloud and Desert Flower, his wife. Only in a few isolated incidents did White Cloud ever even mention the glider or his medical knowledge to his family. The day of the yellow glow had been his experience and his alone. There was a door between the Indians and White Cloud that was ignored at times, moved sometimes, but never traveled through. Desert Flower never expressed any desire to permanently go back to her people. She belonged to White Cloud and with White Cloud she would stay until the spirit world beckoned her.

In the other time I had often heard words like compatibility, or statements like "working out a relationship," or "having things in common." As strange and unnecessary as these statements had seemed to me at times, I will never forget that Indian lady of those beautiful years at the cove. We had compatibility, nothing much in common and our relationship came as natural as everyday living.

As far as I could tell, Desert Flower had been about nineteen years old when she had come to the cove. She was delighted when her hair began to turn white like mine, but in the meantime her face had begun to wrinkle and for that she was quite disenchanted. Grandchildren amongst the Indian tribe had started a change in my name. Oh, I was still White Cloud to them, but an addition had been placed and now I was White Cloud the Eternal One. Desert Flower's younger brother had been chief for many seasons. His hair was white and he could still remember and quote a detailed report of the tribe meeting me in the O'Neil area. They called that place "White Cloud Crossing." They still believed I had the power to go in and out of the spirit world whenever I desired. So that coupled with the fact that I never aged brought them to the conclusion that I had always existed and would always exist.

Every once in a while the question of time would invade my mind and leave me with a restless feeling. The year identification was a knowledge I did not have and although I had often tried to figure it out, I could not come to any concrete conclusions. My first clue came one day when I had taken my glider and had followed the Deschutes River clear to the Columbia River area. It was a blustery day along the big river gorges and within the preceding week I had explored much of the old canyon. At the particular time in mention I had been up a side spur canyon that I identified as that one which in the other time had led down to the Biggs Junction. As I came out of that canyon I saw a small campfire near the river. A lone figure was nearby, and at the distance which I was it did not appear to be an Indian. There were many small bands of Indians that lived along this river and many of them were rather hostile. I had been here on occasions before and I had learned to be very cautious. To see a loner was quite out of character with the area. I had not seen a non-Indian human since my awakening and, though, I could not see this person clearly, the movement and camp arrangement were definitely not Indian. I placed my glider in a growth of small saplings. There was a lot of high brush along the river so I could stay out of sight until I was within a few feet of the camp. My eyes scanned the camp in a quick inventory. There was no horse or any other means of conveyance. Some of the clothing was Indian made and probably acquired by trade.

The man himself was a short stocky black man. His skin was as black as any storm cloud that rolled across the sky. His eyes were narrow and he had a very pronounced wrinkle where the bridge of his nose met his forehead.

I watched the man for some time and was sure he had spent perhaps many years on the move. I was sure also that a great deal of luck and good fortune had traveled with him. Leaving all weaponry he had, he left his simple camp behind him and went to the river for water. Knowing it was time to make my move, if I was going to, I stepped out between the man and his camp. It surprised me that the man never even noticed me until he was about ten feet from me. Perhaps he was very tired, at least I gave him that benefit of the doubt. When he finally looked up, a look of utter shock came across his face.

"Oh laaw, oh laawzy. Misr, Ah dasn't knowd yo. Pleez dona take me back."

His whole countenance began to change as he talked on.

"Isah gonna fat yo ifn yo tra, suh. Ah sho nuff fat yo hod."

The man stood there knowing full well that I had an extreme advantage over him. It occurred to me that with his talk of being taken back, he was probably a runaway slave. If I was right then the year identification could be anywhere from the late sixteen hundreds to the early eighteen hundreds. I hadn't had any clue up to this point and it could have been the year one as far as I knew.

"Sir, I really don't plan on fighting you under any circumstances, nor do I plan on taking you anywhere. My home, my wife and my family are within a ten day foot journey from here, you are welcome as a guest there if you desire, but there are many things I might learn from you and things you might learn from me, as friends."

With his thick accent, I wasn't sure if he would understand me and I knew it was hard to understand him.

"Yo say freen, suh no what man eva wana be freen befo. I wa bone Kavwan of a Sawi tribe when what man's come and cotched me and takes me fa fa away. Isah only seven yeahs ol an they tooks me an sells me to a masah. Ah wook hod but he beetn me most to death. Ten harvests an ah runs away. Ah hasn't foun the Sawi an home, but ah isn't gonna back to them Masah."

"How long have you been gone from your master, Kavwan?" I asked.

"Twenty havasts ago. They calls me African niggah Jim."

"Do you know what year date it was when you left?"

I believe I was shaking with excitement as I listened for his answer. Many questions could be answered for me and it all depended on this man's answer.

"Masah Fugrson sas seventeen fifty havasts gonna be good."

"Is that when you left?'

"Ya suh."

"So if you left in seventeen fifty and have been gone twenty years, this must be the year seventeen seventy."

"Seventeen seventy-one as I know. Does yo be a what Indian suh?"

I have been named by the Indian as White Cloud. Much of my existence has been a mystery. Some of it even to me. I stayed with Kavwan for two days and learned much of his daring escape. How he had laid in the bottom of the Mississippi River for three days breathing through a reed so as to elude those that sought him. He had followed the river upstream sometimes staying in the water for a week at a time. He told me that he stayed in the water so much that he thought his skin would fall off. His was an incredible story that should have been recorded in history. I learned many things from this man and I was able to share some things with him. I know history has a close record of white man's entry and travels in this vast land, but it somehow bypassed White Cloud and the black man and Midwestern part of this continent that any other man on foot could ever cover. It gave me a twinge of sadness to think that he still looked for a passage to Sawi in Africa. If I could have figured out a way to get him there I surely would have. Perhaps he found his way home. I suggested he go into the Eastern Canada area and try to book passage to Africa.

Back at the cove I got out my own calendar and the diary I had kept. According to my calculations my awakening had been in the year of sixteen ninety. Once in a while I would get a flashback sensation of the time before my awakening and would see friendly and hostile faces, jungles and deserts. Sometimes I would see a vast ocean and a ship and feel an urge and desire for home. Meeting the black man had brought back those feelings strong to me, back from somewhere in the foggy past, but they were always relieved when I remembered the day I reached the cove. If Desert Flower had been ten years old when I first saw her at White Clouds Crossing then she was now ninety one. Even in her nineties, though, she was a very active and truly beautiful woman.

The night before there had been a violent thunderstorm that had seemed to have shaken every rock along the canyon. The morning dawned balmy with signs of being a rather warm spring day. Desert Flower had lost her desire to raise early so I tried not to disturb her when I turned to start my log for the day. I entered the date as May 23, 1802. I had stayed pretty close to home for some time. My heart was saddened by the thought, but I knew the spirit world was calling one I had loved longer than most people live.

The sun was well into the sky when Desert Flower sat up on our mat as though she was about to start her day. For some time she just sat there with arms lifted to the sky as though in worship which I was sure was the case in fact. Slowly her arm came down to remove the opal necklace that I had made and placed on her neck over one-hundred years before. Slowly she turned to me.

"Someday when the sun gets too tired to shine and there is no more water to flow in the rivers, when the moon no longer lights the night for the deer to feed. When the mountains have worn down to become part of the desert. At that time the eternal one, my White Cloud will join me in the spirit world. Many people will know White Cloud, both great and small will honor him. My heart desires that he will not forget Desert Flower. Carry this gift with you always to remember Desert Flower."

I was going to answer her and assure her but her body sank into my arms as the spirit world carried the beautiful flower away. I quickly gathered the limp body up in my arms, and with tears streaming down my cheeks I rushed outside hoping her spirit moved slowly on its journey.

"Oh my pure sweet Desert Flower, my precious flower, I will never forget you though the mountains become low and the canyons reverse their thrust and reach for the stars. There will be another star and bright spot in the sky and each time I look heavenward I will see you and remember. Each time new life blooms in the spring, I will remember my flower. Each time another pure snowflake falls to the ground I will know that you gave it an inspiration to beauty. The spirit world has gained a beauty that the world has lost forever."

How long I had stood there with the tears flowing, I don't know, but I soon became aware of people around me. As far as I knew no one had summoned them, but there were my sons, Thunder Cloud and Grey Cloud and their families. Up the hillside about 40 yards away were others that had honored Desert Flower.

I looked at my two sons, who themselves were old men and my look asked the question I could not form.

"The whole body knows when it loses even though it be small like a toe. We will soon go to the spirit world also, but one part of our body is denied that honor and we feel the pain."

There are some things I will never quite understand, but I understood full well that Thunder Cloud had just told me he loved me.

I wrapped the body of my Desert Flower in the hide of a young doe deer and buried her on a knoll overlooking our domain.

CHAPTER FOUR

It had been ten years since I had spent much time at the cove. After Desert Flower went to the spirit world, I felt a desperate loneliness begin to set in. One summer I traveled far north to an area that in the other time was in Canada. I explored the area in Washington where I had been born. During the winters I would travel south.

I had had several occasions where I came across white people. Most of them were trappers and explorers. For about five years I had tried to satisfy the curiosity I had always had concerning my saddle and the inscription on it. My travel was much in the same mode as on the day of my awakening. I had gone back to my campsite near the lava flow, although there was no sign of my ever being there, I tried to remember my trail as I headed south. It was sometimes difficult to sort out familiar areas as being familiar to me before the yellow glow or during my travels in a state of mind that I did not understand. There were numerous incidents, though that almost opened the door of my memory. The first of those incidents occurred near the area of Mount Shasta when I ran across a tribe of hostile Indians. It became obvious to me that there would be no dealing with them and my only chance was to create a disturbance and run for it. As a captive I rode along a narrow hillside trail with them. One brave was ahead of me and he led my pack horse. About ten followed behind. Ahead on the upper side of the trail I saw a windfall tree that still hung onto its butt with only a dried splinter type shaft. The top of the tree lay precariously against the limb of another tree and was pointing slightly uphill, but back toward the way we had come.

It looked to me as though the slightest push on the base of the tree would dislodge the top and bring it crashing down across the trail behind me. I quickly heeled my horse in the ribs and reached for the splinter prop for the dead tree. The tree played its part well with the riders behind me. The rider in front turned quickly to take inventory of the situation and would have challenged my fight for freedom, but the knife, I kept by my side, dampened his spirits and he let me go without saying another word. As though I knew exactly where I was going I headed over the hills to a lava flow area. The flow was crisscrossed with narrow passageways that were no more than ten feet deep. By sitting in a crevice of rock it gave me the advantage of keeping me and my horses concealed and in the meantime observing anyone approaching.

As I sat there it became clear in my mind that once before I had caused some kind of disturbance in a hostile Indian village and had run to this very spot. Where had I been though? How far had I come and how I got there in the first place. Since my awakening I hadn't forgotten one moment, yet between the day of the glow and that there had to have been a lengthy span that to me was shrouded in mystery.

As I sat in the rocks I saw six Indians ride over the hill. With them they led four more that were draped over the horses but that left one unaccounted for. I was uneasy about that until the next day when I rode back past the place I had topped the tree. The lead man was still there even quieter than the last time I had seen him. Perhaps he had been dishonored. Maybe they blamed him for the incident. However, it was, they had left him there. They stopped and looked hard at the lava bed and I'm sure they knew I was there, but they also knew I had the advantage over them so they soon rode off.

That particular trip took me clear to Southern California and into Mexico where I came across a group of missions. I was told that the missions had been established by a priest named Junipero Serra who, according to the accounts I received, was a saint indeed. I stayed with one of the missions for almost a year. Many were the acts of mercy performed by the mission and I felt obligated to use my medical knowledge.

One time a small Mexican girl was brought to me with pain in her lower right abdomen. It was by dark of night after the girl was recovered, that I quietly left the mission and began my journey back northward. The incident had triggered in me again the strong desire to reach home.

Many times I had repaired my glider. I had replaced the skin almost yearly depending on usage. I had tried different materials from time to time, but while I was in or near Mexico I had acquired some silk so I once again reskinned the glider using the silk I didn't know it at that time, but I wouldn't be using the glider much longer.

It was midafternoon on a particular blustery day when I noticed a lone rider coming into the canyon. The horse moved very slowly so I was sure there was no urgency involved.

The old Indian man got off his horse and with his deformed leg, painfully sat on the ground in the place that many times before I had sat in council with the Indians. I sat down in front of him without a word to await his message.

"I am Wounded Eagle. Before my eyes had seen many moons. Before I was old enough for battle, our enemies attacked us. Having no honor they wounded the old and the young. Many of our people went to the spirit world. Our chief sent for White Cloud. White Cloud has good magic. I have seen many moons. I have many children and horses. Now it is time for my journey to the spirit world."

Wounded Eagle was silent again for a while. I remembered the time that I had been sent for and I remembered Wounded Eagle. He could not have been more than four or five years old at the time. His leg had been badly mangled. A horse and rider tore through a teepee in the Indian village. I had done my best to set and splint the leg. I had even, somewhat successfully, done skin grafting on the leg. Wounded Eagle began to speak again.

"Many times Wounded Eagle has watched White Cloud go to the spirit world. Many Times Wounded Eagle has watched the old ones and young warriors go to the spirit world. Maybe Wounded Eagle is too proud. He has had many troubles. He is tired of troubles. Wounded Eagle is now ready to go to the spirit world also. Wounded Eagle will not return like White Cloud."

Wounded Eagle stopped again. He had a request that was hard for him to ask for. I knew what the old man wanted and ethically I should have let him state his own request. He had had a hard life, though. His deformed leg had hindered him in many Indian activities. He had rode well and had done fair as a horseback warrior. I understood his mind. He had never been able to really excel in anything in his long life. He wasn't a great hunter. He hadn't counted much coup as a warrior. If only he could at least excel in his trip to the spirit world, perhaps all would be worthwhile.

"Wounded Eagle would like to go to the spirit world like White Cloud?"

The old man grunted his approval.

"Wounded Eagle must learn the magic in the wings that White Cloud wears, but White Cloud will show him the magic."

Perhaps it would be considered murder on my part and yet I knew the old man didn't have much time and if I could give him this culminating satisfaction it would be worth it all. We both went to the top of the canyon and I showed and demonstrated the operation of the glider to the old Wounded Eagle. A strong wind was blowing so there wouldn't have to be any running for the launch. Wounded Eagle strapped the glider on, turned and smiled at me, and just as a big gust of wind came, leaned forward. I watched the cougar headed glider with Wounded Eagle climb higher and higher until it disappeared into a cloud drifting in a south westerly direction.

I had recorded the coming of the New Year as January 1, 1825. Things had started to change all around. Across the mountains along the Columbia River there were a couple of settlements or forts. I had been to these places and I became known as the white- bearded Indian. No one really avoided me, but I hadn't won any popularity contests either. I was thought to have been an Indian captured white child. No one could figure that out, though, because as far as anyone knew there had been no white people around in the years I was a child. No one asked me my age. They just figured me to be around 50 to 60 years old. I had the face of a much younger person, but my hair and beard being so white made them guess me as older. I had overheard one conversation that came to the conclusion that I was probably in my early 30s and that the horror of my capture and life with the Indian savages had turned me prematurely white haired. I had even heard the stated curiosity about the opal necklace I wore. No one knew where I came from and I made sure no one followed me when I left. The fact of me being an early mountain man had occurred to them, but most mountain men were at least accounted for and information of their past attainable.

It was quite a surprise to me when one early morning I heard a voice hollering, "Hello in the cabin. Hello in the cabin."

The teepee was no longer beside my little rock house. Wounded Eagle had been the last one of the Indians to contact me so the appearance of my camp was very similar to the way it was shortly after I had come to the cove. The year was now 1828 and I was sure whites would soon be infiltrating this part of the country and the more the infiltration occurred the more the Indians would withdraw into their own world.

The man that stood near the river was a short plump man whose attire definitely identified him as a trapper, or mountain man.

"Come on in. I was just fixin' me a meal. You might as well join me."

The man would start puckering his lips a short time before he began to speak. As if to make sure the words were formed properly. In conjunction with puckering his lips, a chubby fist would come up with the forefinger pointing as a gesture of his speech.

"I find it hard to turn down an invitation to a good meal and friendly hospitality. My name is Arron Wilson."

The man continued to talk all the while I was preparing the meal and acting as the host for my guest.

"Long before I was born my father had met a black man and helped him book passage on a ship to Africa, but before the black man left he told my father all about this country. Until the day of his death my father wanted to come and see if it all were like the black man said. I wanted to be a preacher, but I promised him the day he died I would come. So I turned trapper, and fur trader and worked my way out here. I don't know if there be much beaver in these parts, but the country is as fascinating as the black man related to my father."

"If any place in this country has beaver, it would be in the river that flows into this canyon a ways north of here. The head of the river comes out from the black mountain that you can see west and slightly south of here at the top of the canyon."

Arron had begun to sit down on a bench I had made, but immediately stood up and with one leg slightly forward he began to bounce as though his knees were springs under him. This time he didn't pooch his lips to ponder the words he was to say, but his fist came up with his forefinger pointing emphatically.

"Sir, though there be millions of beaver near the black mountain, I won't go back near it ever again, never."

Shocked at his response, I turned questioning.

"What about the black mountain has brought about such fear in you?"

With both fists at the end of bent arms near his chest and the one finger pointing dramatically, he told me a story that brought a lump to my throat. It was a lump of joy for knowing I had been able to fulfill a dream of an old friend of mine.

"I went to the top of the black mountain so I could see a good view of all this country. And that I was able to do, but near the top I found what looked to me like a flying cougar. Now sir you might just take me as mad, but I swear to you that in the clutches of that mysterious creature was the skeletal remains of an old Indian man. I thought that I would release the Indian from the hold of that monster and I done that, but a stiff breeze came and startled that cougar and he began to fly off with me. Now, sir, I've seen eagles fly off with rodents, but this was me heading off down the mountainside over the treetops. I finally let go and went crashing through the trees. I wasn't hurt much, so I cautiously went back to bury the Indian. But I vowed until all prophecy in the Bible's revelation are fulfilled and I know for sure what that beast was, I won't go back near that black mountain."

With that, Arron abruptly sat back down with the assurance of a determined mind and I knew I would not discuss the black mountain with him again.

Wounded Eagle had gone to the spirit world like White Cloud. He would not return for there he was young and strong. Both legs were straight. He walked without a limp and he was honored as a chief for he had entered the spirit world as no one else.

I would see Arron many times again, but his fur trapping days were over. He had fulfilled what he had felt to be an obligation by seeing the country the black man had talked about. The black man must have come up the canyon and observed the mountains and the canyons, but he had not come to my rock shelter. I had seen no evidence of him being near, but his ability to keep undercover and out of sight must have worked for him once again.

When Arron left the canyon he headed west across the mountain to the Willamette Valley to become the preacher he had dreamed of being. He lived a long prosperous, healthy life as a traveling preacher. In his later years he went to Seattle to pastor a church there until he left this old world behind. I often heard him preach of the prophetic beasts and his sermons would be filled with, and inspire, even greater awe and wonder. Even as an elderly patriarch gentleman he would take the stance with one leg slightly ahead of the other while using his knees as springs to bounce on. Chubby little fists at the end of bent elbows would be expressing each thought and word while the right fist produced a pointing forefinger. Perhaps on a ledger somewhere, or maybe on some historical record that is old and yellow with age, is the mention of a long forgotten preacher. It is still a wonder to me as to what quality an individual must possess to make his mark last through time. There were the two men with their Indian lady that traveled from the east along the Columbia River and to the Pacific Ocean and their names are well-known. Their very trail is marked and dated between 1804 and 1806. Another man had explored the canyons trying to find the river sources. I have talked with him briefly as he traveled through, yet in his report he claimed to have encountered nothing but Indian culture. A park was named for him where a bridge was later constructed to cross the narrow canyon of the crooked river. I suppose the fact is that one's like Arron Wilson or the black man or even White Cloud never submitted a written report to any official of the government. If it were within my power to do so, I would bring to the surface of knowledge the facts of the real explorers and brave people of the past. I guess it's similar to the well-known of the other time. I have found some real musicians that were never broadcast as stars or people uneducated in formal accredited schools, but that had an insurmountable amount of wisdom and great gifts of common sense.

Several summers had passed as the present one was about to do, when the site of a lone Indian rider made it seem as though time had again been turned backwards. This time perhaps a hundred or so years. The man rode to and dismounted at the very place where other councils had been held years ago. After the usual time of thought and calling on the Great Spirit for wisdom, the man began.

"I am Summer Cloud the son of Lame Horse, the son of Thunder Cloud. My memory has not failed me for when I was not many summers old I stood on that hillside and watched while White Cloud held the body of Desert Flower and cried to the Great Spirit. Thunder Cloud was good to listen to. Lame Horse found out it was bad not to. I sat in council with Thunder Cloud. He told me many things about White Cloud. He told me of his great wisdom. He told me how White Cloud takes council in the spirit world, and that I would do well to listen to the council. Lame Horse would not listen to White Cloud's wisdom because his skin is not red. Lame Horse says that many white skinned people will come and take away our land and destroy our people."

A strong enemy came far from the south and killed many of our people. We hid in caves to escape them. They were not white skinned.

When we go to the fishing grounds at the big river we see white skinned people and sit in council and hear of many pale skin people as a strong enemy.

"Much of Lame Horse's council was true."

As I sat listening to the lament of this Indian man, a feeling of mixed emotion flooded my mind. This was my great grandson, yet we lived virtually in two different worlds that were becoming more and more distant as time progressed.

The council that I would give Summer Cloud could not lighten his heavy heart, but more than a hundred years later I would see clear evidence that my counsel was kept.

"There are good red men and there are bad red men. There are good pale men and there are bad pale men. The pale man is a very strong enemy. Many red men will fight the pale man and many red men will die. The pale man will take his land and his horses. He will take much of your land also, but many summers from now your people will find wealth in your land and will become strong again. The Great Spirit knows you and your people and will not forget you, and you will always find peace with White Cloud."

Summer Cloud spoke again.

"Thunder Clouds counsel was true."

With that statement Summer Cloud left and as he rode up the canyon, part of my heart and soul went with him. I did not turn back toward my rock cabin until the sun's brightness was only shining on the rim rock at the top of the canyon. I longed to turn around and see Desert Flower beside the teepee, but I knew she would never be there again.

The white man was coming and the land would take many changes. Some of these changes I dreaded seeing, but I did not know how I personally can change the course of time.

CHAPTER FIVE

White people were becoming more prevalent with the Oregon Territory and settlements were becoming towns. There was quite a growing town on the Willamette River named Oregon City and it was there I met a man named Shebbard Douglass. Sheb, as he was known, had come from Great Britain as a child and was orphaned a few years after reaching the colonies. He had worked as a wagon and carriage builder and had eventually come west with a wagon train repairing wheels and wagons on the way. Once in the Oregon Territory, Sheb had become a carpenter and was kept quite busy in the growing communities.

I had gone to Oregon City because Arron Wilson was to be there. He was going to be preaching there and I wasn't going to miss the opportunity to hear him. It was at that meeting house I met Sheppard and we became quite good friends.

Sheb never asked any real vital questions about me, but he and Arron discussed my person several times, always coming to the conclusion that there was something different and special about me, something they could not explain. As far as my background was concerned, to them my name was Dean Williams. I had been raised from babyhood by the Spanish people somewhere in Mexico, and some time as a preteen had left to travel north to the cove where I had found an existence with the Indian as my companions. I knew I had been in Mexico, but in a foggy state of mind. My old saddle was still near my rock cabin with the inscription plainly visible, but the saddle in the neighborhood of two hundred years old wasn't in very good condition. I had also been in and near Mexico for a while after the death of Desert Flower. Some of that foggy time had come to my mind from time to time and I had recorded it as I could, but the complete picture was quite confusing to me.

Sheb had quite an adventuresome spirit about him and so it was when he heard about the discovery of gold in California he wanted to go. And that is how it came about that we both became part of the group known as the Forty-niners.

Sheb approached me quite cautiously at first, inquiring about my knowledge of the California Territory. It would have been far beyond his comprehension if I had told him of driving up and down throughout the whole West Coast in trucks and cars in the other time. I chuckled at the thoughts that race through my mind. Sheb would not live long enough to see those times as they approached again, and in many ways I considered him and the people of those days far more privileged than I.

"I think I have a reasonable knowledge of the area." I answered.

"I have good friends here, but I have good friends in the colonies also. Perhaps I'll never see any of them again, but I have the urge to go."

I could see the wanderlust strong and Sheb's eyes, so wander we would.

I did not plan to take the most direct or quickest route as I wanted to do some more exploring myself. We would travel light and mostly on foot and most of it would be hilly and timbered. Hard winters seem to come in a cycle of three years except that every ten years there would be a break in the cycle and then that year there would be an extremely hard winter. Whereas the winter, that will be approaching, fell within the ten year cycle, we wasted no time in getting underway. I wouldn't be too concerned about the weather after we cross the Siskiyous and we were leaving early enough to do that.

Most of the Willamette Valley was easy travel for along the river were trails becoming well worn by trappers and settlers. I began to hear words about progress and development of the land. Words that made my heart ache with sadness. For many years I have watched nature take its course. I had once seen a growth of timber take on a disease and begin to die. I kept a close watch on the timber area to see how far the disease would spread. Then one particular summer day lightning struck right on the edge of that area. The fire that raged burned out the diseased timber then began devouring the dense underbrush from the surrounding trees.

Within a limited period of time nature's own reforestation program was underway.

I have seen in the desert when rabbits seem to be in an overabundance, how the coyote population would increase. The natural balance of nature had worked for many years on its own and I wondered what development the land needed by the hand of man. The coyote litter changes in number according to the jackrabbit population. Things like this are amazing to study and behold. Although much of my existence I did not understand, I was and still am grateful to have been able to see the handiwork of nature's ways before mankind took over.

We crossed the Siskiyous and came to the Klamath River in the most colorful time of the year. The gold color of fall flashed brightly all around us.

"Sheb, if you want real gold, you can see it here sparkling through the woods."

"I believe, my chap that I can see the very value of which you speak and it would be renewed year-by-year."

We stopped by the river and made a raft of poles to convey us down the river. Mount Shasta looms right before us as it prepared for its new winter's coat of snow. We finally made our launch into the river that led us from the relatively open area into a deep valley with high rolling hills all around us. We hadn't gone very far until I saw something more than halfway up the hillside that put a strange feeling deep in my chest. Sheb had caught the expression change that it had brought about.

"My man, Dean, what is it you see? Pray tell me."

I pulled the raft to the south side of the river and disembarked, then I pointed to the hillside.

"That is what I see, Sheb. I've got to go up there."

"My conscience, my chap, it looks like something took a bite out of the mountain to fill the ravine. I wonder what could have done that."

Since my awakening I had not seen one sign of the other time. I had lived for years in an unhampered-with world. Now seeing this cut in the hillside gives me a fearful sick feeling. I wasn't ready to change back to a modernistic world yet. I'll readily admit there were problems in this life. The death of Desert Flower had almost devastated me. The fact that there were still remnants of my family amongst the Indians and that the coming of the white man had separated me from that life disgusted me.

My wife in the other time had been part Indian but raised in a white world. Because of that she had felt a drawing to the Indian culture but was blocked because of upbringing.

I have not cared to share my past life with anyone, but here on the hillside was a scar that brought back to my mind the freeways roaring with traffic that had crisscrossed the country. I almost expected to look into the sky and see the contrail of a jet.

My race up the hill had left Sheb in a puffing, panting sweat, trying to keep up.

"My Gawd man, that's, I would guess, five or six hundred feet close to straight up or down, and we covered it in less time than a man could travel it at a brisk walk on the land."

Sheb had sat down on the edge of the fill to catch his breath and as he got up he dislodged a boulder from the side. The boulder went crashing down the mountainside causing a miniature slide to go with it. I was about fifty yards away when I saw Sheb pick up something from where the boulder had been.

"Hey, Dean, what in heaven's name is this?"

He handed me the piece of material that he had found.

"It's all flat on one side and has that gold like streak in it. Is it of any value, my man?"

"It's what's called asphalt and no, it's of no value at all."

As I held a piece of asphalt in my hand my emotions went wild. I lifted it above my head and a growling scream came from my throat.

"Why? Why?"

Although I had no right to be, I was angry. The one who had cleansed the earth's surface had left this blemish. Why? Was it to torment me? I threw the piece to the ground and saw it disintegrate before my eyes, just like my television set had in the other time. I looked at Sheb, who by this time, had eyes like a wild man.

"Let's get out of here." I said.

Sheb needed no further suggestion. Without a word he was making huge jumps down the hill, digging his heels into the ground with each leap.

Sheb was waiting impatiently on the raft ready to go when I got there. As soon as we cast off into the middle of the river, the ground began to rumble and shake with the throes of an earthquake. I watched as the cut and fill came cascading down the hill to toss boulders into the river upstream from us. Soon the dust settled and the only sign on the steep hillside was the sign of one of nature's landslides.

Since the day of the yellow glow I had questioned many times what had actually occurred and I suppose I could have counted this incident as a definite blessing for it left in my mind the fact that I had actually lived in a modernistic type world. The incident had created another situation that was to be rather unpleasant for me. Loneliness had been a frequent invader of my existence. Friends like Sheb had been few. The time of the Cloud family in the cove had been a fulfilling time with a total absence of the loneliness that I so often felt, but that had been many years back. Now in this present hour I saw a change come over my good friend Shebbard Douglass. To have been standing in his shoes through it all must have been quite mind-boggling to say the least. I wouldn't have you condemning Sheb for he was a fine gentleman indeed, but the next time he spoke to me was in the evening of the third day later.

"I have not meant to be rude dear Sir, but I am indeed a plain and simple man born of plain and simple parents. I was raised with strong biblical upbringing. I do not claim to be a scholar, yet up until the present I have had few questions concerning the existence of God and the creation of man or the relationship of either. Some have said that, the man Lazarus, whom the Lord raised after being four days dead, still lives today. Perhaps you are that man. I do not know. But I do know that I am not as you and you are not as I."

I knew I did not possess the wisdom to approach the conversation in a manner that would be satisfying to Sheb.

"Perhaps you were correct in the fact that my existence is not as your existence, yet I too am a plain and simple man born of plain and simple parentage. I too was raised with strong biblical upbringing. I only request that until you fully understand my existence and have the answers to time and eternity that you not mention the incidence you have observed or discuss my existence with anyone you might meet."

He did not honor that request.

From that moment the close companionship with Sheb ended. Sheb treated me with a reverent awe referring to me as sir.

While many others searched for the mother lode, my route to the gold fields purposely took us down the Klamath River then up the Eel

River through the giant sequoia Redwoods. Sheb lost much of his lust for gold as we lost ourselves in the, at the time, virtually untouched redwoods.

"Sir, I do believe that if it be agreeable to you, after we have seen Yerba Buena, I shall return here. I believe with all the people coming to this area many homes will be needed. Maybe I can contribute to my fellow man by producing the lumber for such. I do believe this is where the Almighty would have me labor the rest of my days."

Yerba Buena, or San Francisco, as it is more lately called, was nothing in comparison to the San Francisco I had been in on numerous occasions in the other time. Quite active for sure, yet it was not near the size of the modernistic San Francisco I had known. It had been raining for a couple of days before Sheb and I arrived, so the streets were deep with mud. The mud, though, did not seem to slow the scurry and bustle of many would be rich men. It soon became apparent that many had spent all they had to get to this destination and so were destitute in an environment that was strange to them. I also found myself in a situation that I had not faced since the other time. I had lived quite comfortably and yet never with any money. Money would have been useless to me even though I'd have had mountains of it. In San Francisco money was needed to exist. Sheb rented a small room over a saloon which we were to occupy for a couple of weeks, then he set out to contact lumber men to go into business with him back in the Redwoods. The saloon beneath our room had an old upright piano with the typical old west saloon sound. One evening as I was walking through, the saloon keeper hollered out that he needed someone to take the job of playing the piano for the saloon. It really wasn't a job that appealed to me a great deal, but I thought that it might be somewhat enjoyable for a time. Besides it seemed no one else could play at all. In the long run it became quite rewarding.

Two weeks quickly passed and Sheb was ready to leave San Francisco. Things were looking quite well for him and he was to become a well-known and well-to-do logging and lumber man.

"Dear, sir," he addressed me one morning. "I am rather concerned with your future. Don't take me wrong, for I know that you are perhaps far more adequate than I to handle any situation that would come your way, but I feel that I will not see you again for a long time and maybe never in this life. You see, sir, feeling rather inadequate myself, I would feel much better if I knew of your future and where you might be. Will you be going back to the Oregon Territory?"

"Not for a while, Sheb, but eventually, yes. The canyons will always have a drawing to me. They have been home to me for many years. I believe, though, that I will seek passage around the Horn and go back East for a spell. I will miss you, Sheb, for you have been a true and close friend. That, in itself, has been a very rare treat for me. I am truly sorry that my own background and emotional tantrum on the river has brought about our separation, but go with God, my friend."

Sheb stood looking at me for some time with tears slowly moistening his face. He then slowly turned and walked out the door and I was never to see him again. I believe my emotions have a proper balance, yet as I sat there I had the same feeling of loss and loneliness come over me as when I had buried Desert Flower on the knoll behind my rock shelter in the Crooked River Canyon.

I had gotten quite the reputation during the short time I had been playing the piano in the saloon. I played many of the tunes that I remembered from the other time and it was thought that the songs were of my own composition. Surely, I must be a well-educated man and so it was, that I was an approached one evening and asked if I could read well.

"Yes, I believe that I can." I replied to the man before me.

"My name is Jason Brown and I am from New York. I receive a newspaper from home rather regularly. Whereas many people here are from the East. I have found a growing interest in the news from home. I myself do not read well, but I have acquired a building where for a fee, the people can hear the news and then afterwards I sell the paper by the page. To be honest, sir, I was ready to die until I found this way of acquiring funds. I believe I will start a news center here and produce a paper, but in the meantime I would be willing to pay you $100 a reading."

Little by little I began to see the possibilities of obtaining passage around the Horn. The time of my existence before my awakening was foggy in my mind indeed. I had recorded every detail that came to mind, but yet there was much to be filled in. The contrast between the before and the after was staggering. As I have said before, since the time of my awakening I have not forgotten even one second or minute detail of my existence. I remembered ditching the ship as I had sailed around the Horn before. Had not the ship set anchor somewhere else on the continent that would have been much closer to my goal and home? How had I survived or found my way through the jungle and rugged terrain of South and Central America? How long had I existed in a foggy state of mind. These thoughts were constantly in my mind and it was these very thoughts of mystery that had driven me to the Mexican Territory years before.

Well, I have done it once again. My mind has wandered from the track of my document. Back at the saloon in San Francisco, though things were rather typical. Very often some fellow would enter flashing his sack of gold dust around which usually ended in a fight. I did not involve myself in the inebriation or the fights of the saloon. I had always enjoyed music the other time and this time, and I usually just tended to my own business. One night, though, a man came in with excitement and anticipation written all over him. He had struck it rich some one hundred miles or so to the east. He had sent for his family including a young bride and they were to arrive by ship the next day. He had invited the rest present to help him celebrate this good fortune and excitement. I had taken notice of another man that had frequented the saloon. A ne'er-do-well type that seemed to be on a constant look for trouble. He was a rather small man with a black wiry beard. His jaw was noticeably offset by injury rather than by defect. I had also noticed that there was a bulge at his side under his top coat that he always wore and I knew he carried a gun.

He had accepted a drink paid for by the younger man and demanded another. When the drink was denied he threw himself into a corner and drew his gun.

"George Bronson, you're a claim jumper. That gold is mine, so hand it over or I'll spill your brains on the floor."

The little man had pulled his hat low over his beady eyes. His raspy voice demanded attention.

"My name is Timothy Lautter and I have never seen you before." the young man answered.

"I'm Mike Chesterfield, you rotten coward. You killed my brother and jumped our claim."

Perhaps Mike had had a bad experience, but this was obviously a mistaken identity. Anger and strong drink had control of Mike's ability to reason. I soon saw his thumb start to reach for the gun's hammer and a vision of a cougar's leap for my horse flashed in my memory. Again my speed was as lightning and my aim accurate. My knife had ripped from its scabbard and had jerked Mike's gun hand back, nailing it by coat sleeve to the wall. The shot fired by, the gun tore a slice down Mile's leg.

I took the gun from Mike and released his arm then began treating the wound on his leg. Mike was still cursing the George Bronson who had done him wrong.

Most had gone back to normal saloon activities, but several men stood around in amazement at the speed of my knife and the treatment of Mike's leg. One of those that stood by was the young man, Timothy Lautter, although he never spoke a word.

"I'll kill Bronson, I swear if it's the last thing I do." The little man growled on.

"You might have just cause for your anger, Mike, but you'll have to realize that the man you're looking for is not here."

Mike looked at me with his beady eyes seeming to have the power to bore holes.

"Well, where in hell is he then?"

"I'm sure I wouldn't know," I answered. But if he is in hell, you'll end up living with him going the way you are."

I had finished with Mike's leg, having put in several stitches and then bandaging it, so with that he limped out of the saloon. The following day I was invited to the morgue to identify a man that in a drunken stupor had stepped out in front of a fast moving wagon near the docks. A black bearded man with an offset jaw and bandaged leg.

The next evening as I was playing for the saloon, Timothy came and asked me if I could leave and follow him. Fearing no harm I followed him to the hotel where he introduced me to his young wife and elderly parents.

"This is the man I told you about. I don't know his name, but every detail of the incidents I shared with you is true."

The elderly man extended his hand.

"Your name sir?" he questioned.

"My name is Dean Williams. I come from Oregon Territory."

The elderly Paul Lautter dominated the conversation for a while.

"Mr. Williams, I am pleased to make your acquaintance. By what my son has told us, I do believe you saved his life. Now sir, I am disappointed that my son would visit a drinking house as I am a godly man."

"A Methodist." interrupted Mrs. Lautter.

"Yes, a Methodist, my dear. You see sir, we have been farmers near Atlanta, Georgia, but not holding to the idea of slavery. We have been poorly. We have discussed the idea of rewarding you as my son has done real well, but as a frequenter of a drinking house yourself, I questioned...."

Paul Lautter trailed off giving me a chance to answer the questions on his mind.

"I too, am a godly man, sir," I began. Mrs. Lautter interrupted again.

"Are you also Methodist, sir?"

"I was reared with Biblical teachings, although I hold to, nor reject any particular church established teachings. A friend and I had rented a room over the saloon. I had not lived with a need of currency exchange until I came to San Francisco, so when the music job was offered it became the means for a meager existence."

"Are you a doctor?" Mr. Lautter asked.

"Man, I do not claim to be a doctor, but living away from any civilization, as I have, one learns by necessity."

"Would you leave the saloon if we reward you then?" Timothy asked.

"I have been hoping to acquire enough to book passage around the horn."

Mrs. Lautter turned pale.

"Sir, that most definitely is a hard trip. I would not do it again. I will die in California."

A discussion therefore began centering around the comparison of a trip by land or sail. Timothy had come by land with an inexperienced wagon master. Most of the people of the original wagon train had died either by Indian attacks or by the lack of water crossing the deserts. Timothy and five other men had left the survivors at Fort Laramie and had struck out alone for California.

"I want you to know that I have not sought for reward. I have only done what seemed necessary at the time."

Timothy had answered me that it was that action that he felt both obligated and privileged to reward.

"I only wish you could have been with us coming west. I know many lives would have been saved," he had added.

I accepted that reward which not only financed my voyage, but supported me for some time thereafter.

I did not have to worry about packing many possessions, just my bed role, and a few necessities placed in a backpack. As I left the saloon and headed toward the shipping docks I blended in with most of the others along the muddy streets of San Francisco in the other time. What a variety there was then. The well-dressed business executives to the unkempt hippie. Of course with my long beard and backpack I probably looked more like the hippie element of the other time, and yet I was accepted as a mountain man or explorer. Here, to, you could tell the novice and newcomers from the hardened proprietor. It was also apparent by appearance, those who had come by land or by sea.

I thought it quite appropriate that I booked passage on a clipper ship named *The Flying Cloud.* Did the lingering existence of White Cloud invade this situation also? The sailing vessels were impressive as they lined the busy and cluttered docks. *The Flying Cloud* was to sail early the next morning and I was told the trip would take eighty nine days plus eight hours.

I was preparing to embark when a constable cautiously approached me.

"Are you Dean Williams?" he asked.

"That I am," I replied. "And what pray tell can I do for you?"

"Do you go by another name, Mr. Williams?"

"In the Oregon Territory the Indians christened me White Cloud. I have gone by the name White Cloud more years than I have gone by my given name."

"Tell me sir, does the questioning of my identity have anything to do with the man, Mike Chesterfield?"

I could not fathom the idea of the questioning, but the thought of Shebbard came to my mind also. Was he in trouble or in need of my help in some way?

"I was told of the incident with Tim Lautter and Mike Chesterfield. I was also told, in a very graphic manner, of your outstanding abilities and comprehension of people and situation to no small degree. I had become acquainted with the man Shebbard Douglass. I shared with him of our catastrophic needs in the law enforcement of this area. I am, in fact sir, prepared to offer you a position as a law enforcement officer."

The man that stood before me was the very epiphany of despair. The job before him in this rapidly growing Bay City was out of control.

The vigilantes took the law into their own hands and left the established law enforcement as a non-entity. People were being kidnapped and shanghaied to serve as slaves. Murders and muggings were a constant occurrence. I was fully aware of the dilemma before the constable. I was also aware that the law enforcement in this city would be just as demanding a hundred or more years from that point in time. Through the years there would be an army of unsung heroes that would give their lives to a job that would never be completed. The life of the constable that stood before me hung on a fragile thread. The armies Presidio was of some help, but their obligation was mostly military. I, myself, who stood with great advantage of offering the world something of lasting value had no desire to do so in this manner. If I could inspire others to greatness or warn of evils to come so that some might evade the trauma. This would be my purpose fulfilled.

"Perhaps more so than you will ever realize, I understand your dilemma, sir. Perhaps I also have abilities that would be advantageous to you, but I have no desire to stay on the Barbary Coast. San Francisco will continue to grow and one day this whole bay area will all be city. The need for law enforcement will increase, but I cannot be tied down to such a city life. I hope you understand, sir."

I'm sure he did understand, to some degree, but he was a man that thrived on challenge. Although I met him only on that one short encounter, he has stood forth in my mind as another one that should have been remembered in the annals of history.

CHAPTER SIX

Although I had never been a sea type individual, even in the other time, I had been greatly fascinated by the old sailing ships and had wanted to experience being on one. *The Flying Cloud* was not old by any means. Everything seemed to be, as it were, shipshape. I was assigned a cubicle for sleeping below deck that would accommodate my pack and enough room to turn over occasionally.

The creaking of the timbers with the swaying of the ship was as I had long imagined. I enjoyed watching the high masts with the billowing sails and standing beneath them gave me a feeling of awe as did the high canyon walls of home. The sea-hardened sailors with muscles bulging went about their tasks with precision, but the sound of a steam or diesel driven engine was not to be heard.

As I stood on the dock, watching the rolling sea, my mind suddenly flashed back to a time before I was a deckhand waiting for the time when soon we would see land. That land would be the southern tip of the new continent that would connect me with home.

A fellow sailor stood on that deck telling me about that continent and his story was filled with wild imaginations and superstition.

"The land be filled with giant women. They be blond big breasted women that be cannibals. They start to love you and then they eat you. And they be birds there that be as big as this ship. I've seen 'em carry off sailors like a hawk would carry a mouse. They also be rivers of pure liquid gold. I talked with a pirate that see it, but barely escaped alive. He changed his ways 'cause of the horrors he seen. The wind always blow and the sea be rough every time we pass. The devil he be in that land."

He talked on as we passed the rocky crags of the Strait of Magellan, but I heard no more. I dove over the rail and into the churning sea. When I climbed up on the rocks I watched the galleon sail out of sight.

How had I reached Oregon and how long had it taken? Perhaps I had built a hang glider then too. In my store of memories from that foggy period of time I did recall sailing alone in a small crudely built boat. I also remembered times when on foot I struggled through rugged mountain ranges or dense jungles. I remembered running from a cannibalistic tribe of people, but they were small and mostly men.

Even now as I stood on the deck of *The Flying Cloud* rounding the horn these thoughts raged through my mind. To be honest I once again felt the urge to jump in, but I stood firm. Perhaps the story of a lost period of time would never be completely clear, but to jeopardize the present to pursue the elusive seemed absurd.

It amazed me that a vessel depending on the wind for its power could be so precise in timing, but we docked in New York City within a few minutes of the prescribed time of travel.

As I left *The Flying Could,* I really wasn't sure what I was going to do. Perhaps I would join a wagon train heading West, but the excitement of being part of a history that I had only read and dreamed about in the other time intrigued me. I felt in no real hurry so I would take life as it came. I felt no desire to tie myself down to tasks like the one offered in San Francisco, though.

The streets of New York were rather different from those of San Francisco - this city, although growing, had been established many years before. The streets themselves were mostly cobblestone. The people were well dressed. With men in their tall top hats and the ladies in their bonnets, I stood out like a sore thumb in my buckskins. The attitude toward me was a contrast between an ignoring to an almost reverent awe. The early frontiersman explorer was looked upon as a tough breed for sure. He dealt with Indians that to most in New York were subhuman savages that they had little or no contact with.

The problems of the far away western frontier was of a secondary concern on the minds of these Easterners. The number one topic of conversation was the rising conflict of slavery and southern independence.

I happened to walk by a big church in New York and was intrigued by an inscription that claimed it to be the first Methodist church in America built in the year of 1768. I thought of the Elder Mrs. Lautter and her fascinating devotion with the Methodist.

I also found interest in a notice that a tent meeting was to be held in the park with the evangelist August Ford.

I had heard about the shouting Methodist and I wanted to go and see if it was as I had been told.

I hadn't really been sure of what denomination or church group Arron Wilson was associated with, if any. It really didn't matter to me. Mrs. Lautter had been the first one that I had come in contact with, in this now time that had separated themselves due to a certain doctrine.

I arrived at the park at the opportune time to help set up the large tent. They had a special semi-circular wall that set up behind the platform that acted as a sounding board to help amplify the voice of the speaker. They also had a camp meeting pump organ.

August Ford had fiery red and curly hair and had the character of an early day camp meeting evangelist. As I began to wander through the area out of curiosity the red haired evangelist approached me with a voice that resonated off the trees and buildings.

"Mountain man, you can help over here. It's God's work you know?"

With a demanding authority he marched me to the place they were erecting the tent.

As we approached the tent another man engaged himself in a conversation with the reverend that intrigued me.

"Have you ministered in the South, Brother?"

"That, I have, not fearing wrath or condemnation, I have preached the power of the Almighty to those in the South. Yes, sir, and many have turned from their wayward route." the optimistic evangelist was questioned again.

"Oh, Brother, that is good news for sure, but the church is being split so many ways due to the slavery issue. Even now, sir, there are the Methodist Episcopal, the Methodist Epsicopal South, and the Wesleyan Episcopal. The Word surely says, 'A house divided against itself will fall.' What is to become of us, Brother?"

For a moment, August Ford was taken back, but regained his composure rather quickly.

"Brother, the Word also tells us, "If the son therefore, shall set you free, ye shall be free indeed." If you are bound by these fears they will rob you of your salvation. God will uphold the truth with a strong arm for sure."

I was pressed upon my mind to think of the other time when there were so many church divisions that it seemed ridiculous for sure. I know that even here in the New York time the church was already divided many ways. My own mind seemed divided in many directions also, although I was living in the past, as compared to the former time, yet my mind was also drawn to a past that I had spent in a foggy state of memory. The inquisitive is not to be condemned, I suppose, yet I wondered if my own nostalgia, as I stood working at the little mill, had caused me to be where I was. If I had been satisfied and accepted the way things were, would life have gone on as normal? How can one accept things though, when he sees them as destructive to the future? The man that spoke to the evangelist saw destructive forces in mass against his future. He had spoken to the man that he thought might have the authority to bring about a peaceful solution to his fears.

Maybe a lesson we all need to learn is to speak up. Do something, Get involved when we see injustice in progress. I remembered a news report from the other time about a woman that had been stabbed to death while thirty-nine witnesses stood by not wanting to get involved.

Would the evangelist get involved? Would he use his influence to take hold of the challenge and turn the tide of time?

For this moment, he had made his statement of faith, and turned to walk away, too busy to further involve himself with the matter at hand.

I was most definitely impressed with the Methodist tent meeting. It reminded me of some of the Pentacostal meetings I had attended in the other time. These were truly the shouting Methodist and their exuberance was the fuel that August Ford thrived on. He paced back and forth like a caged animal, preaching with such force that it seemed it would be impossible to excel, but then numbers of the audience would jump to their feet, shouting, waving and dancing about which would create an even greater crescendo.

I was about to leave the meeting area, not sure where my route might take me, when I was approached by a man that appeared to be quite wealthy.

"It would be a sheer pleasure for me to make your acquaintance sir, for I am truly fascinated with the strength, endurance and wisdom of the men of your caliber."

"Well, sir, my name in a white man's world is Dean Willaims. However in the Oregon Territory amongst the Indians I was known as White Cloud. A name I enjoyed going by."

"Have you therefore been a trapper, Dean?"

I could sense the questions of my origin about to emerge, so felt an evasive answer might be useful.

"No, sir. Much of my origin is not clear in my own mind but I have spent much of my existence in the Oregon Territory with Indians there. I have explored much of this frontier, though.

The gentleman's countenance changed to some degree. Although there was no less amount of fascination, there now came a curiosity that he knew would, perhaps, not be satisfied.

"Well, Mr. White Cloud, perhaps I ought to introduce myself, for I have been rather rude, I'm afraid. I am Jack Jason Benton and I have been in the trading business. The Bay Company has depleted the beaver market to quite some extent. Many men like yourself have found it difficult to succeed in the beaver pelt trade. I am now involved in the market of the buffalo hide. There is great wealth to be obtained for a tough breed of men as yourself."

"Mr. Benton, I really don't mean to be detrimental to your business, but the beaver will multiply again after a given period of time. The buffalo, however, will be diminished to almost extinction. Their return will probably never be again as it has been.

I am aware of white man's desire to control the Indians by the destruction of the buffalo, but I believe there are peaceful ways of bringing that about also.

You see sir, I also think of future generations that will either benefit or be deprived by our decisions now.

"I, myself, have lived quite comfortably with my needs being met in abundance. Yet until recently money in great quantity would have done me no good. Maybe someday my existence will require a job of some kind, but not yet."

Mr. Benton stood stroking his chin for some time before he made any reply.

"My! I am rather taken back by your wisdom and insights and would probably do well to heed to your advice. Beyond the obvious, though, I do detect something outstandingly different about you. Are you therefore in New York in search of your origin?"

"I would have to say that my coming around the horn did have a multi-purpose, but yes, part of that purpose is the search for my origin. Another desire on my mind is to get a better perspective of the thought pattern that is prevalent here in the East, concerning some of our problems in a fast changing western frontier. If I can do anything to help preserve the culture and heritage of the territories then I will certainly do that. The mass slaughter of the Indian, the buffalo or, even the timber there, is not the answer."

A look of disbelief went skipping across Mr. Benton's features but was followed eagerly by an even greater curiosity.

"Oh my man, Mr. Williams, do you also see the vast expanses of timber in the west as also threatened?"

"I understand your shock at my statement, but don't you suppose that soon the train tracks will provide much greater access to the West? When that occurs many people will migrate west. Land will be cleared and homes built."

"Oh no, perhaps not in our lifetime as we see it, but yes, that day will also come."

"Ah, Mr. Williams, now I understand. How could I have missed it having just attended a meeting such as this?" As Mr. Benton talked, he gestured dramatically.

"You, sir, are surely a prophet."

It was getting rather late by the time Mr. Benton bid me a fond adieu,

Not knowing what new adventures were held in store for me as a new day arrived, I rented a hotel room in New York City and dreamed of the Cloud family at the cove in days gone by.

Another day did dawn. A day that was rather unusual to me, not only in the fact of a vastly different environment, but a day that would bring new revelations to me.

I had gone to a restaurant to order a meal to start the day when my mind transformed me to another time. I sat in a similar but cruder establishment. Facing me across a plank table was a lady who had experienced the same yellow glow scenario that I had. We both realized that our minds had been greatly affected, that we were different than the other people around us. Due to our similarity we had decided to stay together. In the time before the yellow glow she had been in, of all places, New York City, but now we were in Germany speaking the German language. I suppose the reason for that was both of our heritage was of German descent.

I felt a gentle tapping on my shoulder. A lady and gentleman stood looking at me greatly concerned.

"Are you alright, sir?"

I was alright except for the fact that my mind was whirring with numerous facts and various forms of information that I must record.

"Well, yes, I am ok, I believe. I have just let my mind concentrate on things of the past that are of great concern to me. I have not meant to alarm anyone."

Introducing themselves as Don and Beth Brookshire the gentleman spoke again, "Whereas my wife's sister had gone to the western frontier some time ago, we had taken special note of you sir. I have also just finished my studies to become a doctor so seeing you sit for quite a time with a blank stare and looking rather pale, I became concerned."

As they both set themselves at my table, Beth began to talk of her sister.

"My sister, sir, married a young man by the name of Timothy Lautter, who shortly after their wedding headed west with a wagon train. We did not hear from him for over two years. He then sent money so that my sister and her in-laws could join him in the California Territory. I do miss her greatly, sir."

I had heard the statement, "it's a small world," which seemed appropriate at that time. It turned out to be a joyous occasion for them as I shared about my having met Timothy Lautter.

"Well, this is a coincidence for sure, just before my booking passage around the Horn. I had met Timothy Lautter, his wife and his family."

Beth Brookshires could hardly keep her lady-like composure and asked for each little detail of information that I might have.

Upon telling of the incident with Mike Chesterfield, Don Brookshire became rather interested in my medical background. He had asked about the extent of my practice. I told him of the appendectomy performed on a young Indian girl, the removal of the arrowhead from the hip of Grey Wolf and the attempt in repairing Wounded Eagle's leg.

I never told him how many years ago that had been or he surely would have taken me as mad. Don asked me what form of anesthetic I had used. When I told him of the mixture the Indians had called "sleeping water", I thought that he would be overtaken by the same symptoms I had had that brought him to my table.

I was fully aware of the nature of the next questions I was to be asked and wasn't sure that I would be able to satisfy his curiosity.

"Where, Dean, and when did you take your medical training? Anesthesia is relatively new, but I have the feeling that you have used it for years. I do believe your name should be down in the annals of medical history."

I most certainly did not want to blatantly lie to Don, nor did I feel justified in telling him the truth of my past.

"Sir," I began. "Years ago I had gotten involved in a group of missions in Mexico and in California. It was there that I got involved in many medical mercies. It was also there that I ran across a book of medical practices to which I added my own findings and interpretations. I do not believe the book emphasized sanitation enough at all. I observed a man being operated on for a gunshot wound. The one performing the surgical procedure was coughing and sneezing, but wore no facial mask. The patient died a few days later with a violent fever, having taken on much coughing and sneezing."

"Do you therefore wear a facial covering while you do surgery or just when you have a cold?"

Don Brookshire certainly had a very inquisitive and brilliant mind. Although he had completed his formal schooling, yet he was still eager to learn.

"I believe we transmit disease from one body to another if we are not most careful. I'm sure you have observed doctors going from one patient to another without cleaning their hands. I'm sure also that you have observed how many of those patients have mysteriously died when the medical personnel have believed their treatment would be successful."

With great exuberance Don leaned forward as a starving man begging for a morsel of bread.

"Sir, I believe you to be most correct. I don't fully understand why, but it does stand to reason. If this theory is correct then our surgical and medical utensils should also be cleaned."

"In boiling water." I nodded.

"I have studied the findings of scientists such as Robert Choch and Joseph Listing who spoke of bacteriology."

Well I believe that this conversation will be of a great help to me in my own practice. I most assuredly will employ these methods."

Don paused a short while and then began again.

"Dean I believe with the ever increasing conflict between the North and the South that we are going to end up with a battle on our hands. I have been raised in the South, but have received my training in the North. I am preparing my departure to Kentucky and my home where I will begin my practice. I am rather neutral as far as the conflict is concerned, yet I will probably be involved as a medical man. Even without the conflict my workload will be overbearing. I do need help and would be pleased to have you come with me."

"I suppose there would be no harm in me checking it out. I feel no ties with New York. There was an individual that lived here in another time, but I've been out of touch for so long I'm not even sure they're here now."

We would be traveling to Kentucky by way of train and by stagecoach, but before we left New York I bought a suit of clothes that would not set me apart so drastically.

While riding on the train I had time to record my flashback. I had not thought about it for some time, but on the day of the yellow glow I had laid down under a tree and thought I had dreamed. I tried to remember that dreamy state of mind now and it all began to make sense. Probably I had been transported to Germany while I was suspended in the yellow glow. If so, then my going home was more than likely a vision of the decay and changes that were taking place.

Then I recalled how, that in the dream, I had been with that woman for five hundred years. Estimating the time it might have taken me to get back to Oregon and adding the five hundred years to that, I figured the world must have been thrown back to the year 1000. My awakening must have been in the 1690 by my calculations. The woman's disappearance after the 500 must have been due to her awakening time. I really didn't have all the facts put together, but the idea was about as much as my finite mind could handle.

CHAPTER SEVEN

I suppose I had, in a way, lost track of time as I worked with Don and Beth Brookshire. We were kept quite busy for sure. We worked out of Don's little farm home on the Kentucky River as it came from the Appalachians.

Many times we were called on to do the veterinary work as well as the treating of sick human bodies. Many were the farms in the region.

There was a time when I became unpopular to say the least. Tobacco was the primary crop and we were treating many of the elderly for a disease that I told Don was called emphysema. I had talked Don into doing a couple of autopsies to compare the lungs of a smoker to the lungs of a non-smoker. Don was amazed at the black ugliness of the diseased lung.

The problem of the Southern Independence and the slavery issue grew increasingly with each day. Many, like Don and Beth, had tried to remain neutral on the subjects, but as time went on the neutrals were looked upon with as much scorn as those with opposite persuasion.

Don had predicted that he would be called on to serve in the military due to his medical knowledge and so it was. The Union Army drafted him to serve as a doctor with a field hospital so he would be moving around much of the time. I remember the date he was drafted as September of 1861.

Beth and I were to try and keep up the practice where we were, but Beth on the other hand wanted to be near as she could to wherever Don would be. Closing out the practice gradually took almost a year. At that time we found out that Don would be in Perryville, so we packed our belongings into Don's buggy and left the little farm on the Kentucky River. I had really enjoyed my time there for several years and with a busy schedule had learned by my involvement.

We heard the devastating roar of war long before we reached the battlefield. The noise did not defer Beth's desire to reach Don though, so we drove on. It was hard to believe the sight before our eyes. The screams and agony of hand to hand combat coupled with the roar of the Howitzer and rifle fire.

As we sat in the buggy wondering what our next move would be, Beth screamed out, "There's Don."

Don was about seventy-five yards away with his arms around a wounded man trying to get him to safety. Beth jumped from the bugg and began to run toward Don. I secured the horse and began to run also, but then I saw a cannon blast hit near to where Don was that obscured him from sight. When the dust and smoke cleared I could not see Don. Beth continued to run then I saw her body jerk, slump and then fall. When I reached the sight, Beth lay about five feet from where Don's dismembered body had come to rest. Beth had taken a rifle shell in her side. That must have passed through her heart. I had turned Beth over hoping there would be something I could do when a confederate soldier came to where I was.

"I...I---didn't mean to shoot a woman sir." When I looked up at him I saw a childlike fear of the young man that stood there. He slowly ventured to look at Beth and then a look of horror and shock came over him.

"Beth," he screamed.

"I shot my own sister. Oh, Beth."

He had taken Beth's body in his arms and was sobbing uncontrollably when a sergeant came by and roughly booted him.

"Come on soldier, let's move."

Quickly the young man reached for his pistol and left a hole in the back of the retreating sergeant's head. He then swung around and turned the pistol on me.

"Get me out of here now, stranger."

We raced for the horse and buggy. Where he was having me go, I had no idea, but the horse was almost wasted and the day far spent by the time he let me slow down. We walked the horse then far into the night until we came to a barn. By this time I had learned that his name was Ted Hartly. He had grown up, like Beth, in a preacher's home and had not lived a violent life. Having, through the line of duty, killed his own sister, his mind had snapped.

"You can bed down in the barn."

I wasn't sure what Ted's intentions were, but I went into the barn and found a mound of hay to lay in where the drastic events of the day tormented me.

I woke up with the pressure of cold steel against my neck. When I opened my eyes I looked up at a Confederate officer who held his finger on the trigger of his rifle.

"You tell me where Ted Hartly is and I'll let you live, old man."

My right arm lay across my chest so with a quick reflex and a twist of my body the projectile went into the hay near my side. With the leverage of the gun, to my advantage, the officer soon found that we had switched places.

"Point number one, sir. I don't know where Ted Hartly is. Point number two, sir, I think you misjudged me. Point number three, sir, I really don't believe you have that authority of whether I live or die."

"I am Colonel Strickland and I have authority from the general to bring in Ted Harlty. He shot Sergeant Garfield in the back for no reason and then deserted. He was with you the last time he was seen."

"Colonel Strickland, I was there and the killing of the sergeant wasn't a no reason incident. Wars' effect on the mind is never a no reason situation. The things that happened yesterday tore a hole in Ted's mind as truly as the bullet in the sergeant's head. Tore a hole in his physical brain, but I am not at fault and if you will realize that fact I'll let you up."

The colonel did get up, but a trifle more cautious than he was before. The incident in the barn had taught him one of life's many wisdom lessons.

As we stood there a man burst through the barn door with a rifle in his hand.

"What is going on in here and who are you two? My name is Jack Hartly and this is my barn. State your business and clear out."

Colonel Strickland told Jack Hartly what had happened the day before and I filled in the details.

"Ted is my nephew and Beth was my niece. Ted is not a murderer, Colonel. He is not here to my knowledge, but if he was, you wouldn't get to him without a couple slugs from my rifle in your body. Now clear out, Colonel."

The colonel left, but I had the feeling I would see him again.

"Is this Doc Brookshire's buggy then?" Jack asked as we left the barn.

The buggy stood without a horse, but otherwise as I had left it.

Jack explained that Ted's parents lived about thirty miles south, near Nashville and suggested we go there immediately. Hooking up his own horse to the buggy we left to make a fast trip. When we arrived we found out that we were only just a few minutes behind the colonel, but that Ted had changed horses several hours earlier. Don's horse had been run so hard that it had died shortly after Ted had left.

Beth had written her parents about me several times so they were well aware of who I was.

Their loss of Beth and their belief that they would never see their daughter again that had married Timothy Lautter was a hard load to bear. They believed that their son Ted would probably go to California to see his sister there.

I became interested when they told me of their plans to go hear an evangelist by the name of August Ford.

"Are you Methodist as were the Lautters?" I asked.

"We are Holiness, but in these days when people are being divided, we believe God's children should gather together."

And so it was that I attended another August Ford meeting. I was rather amazed at the differences in his approach on the slavery issue being in the South as opposed to being in the North.

"The children of Israel were enslaved in Egypt, but it was God that led them to freedom. Jesus said, "I will set the captive free." We need to sit back and let God lead. Too many times men take things in their own hands and mess things up. Let God lead us, let God lead us, let God lead us."

As before August Ford had caused a great crescendoing exuberance in his audience.

The evangelist emphasized the fact that the president of the North was trying on his own merit to set the captive free and that he believed that action to be out of the will of God.

Many were the aching hearts at that meeting. Many had lost loved ones due to the war, so the James Hartleys were able to blend in and feel a comforting for their own souls.

As I left the meeting place, evening was coming on at a fast pace. I came across a farm and I ask the owner if I might spend the night in their barn. The barn was offered for as long as I might need it, but a crippled boy of about eighteen had some things in the barn that he felt impelled to discuss with me. He first took me into a small shop area that he called his laboratory where he had quite a display of birds that he had stuffed and preserved. He also had numerous drawings that depicted his theories of why the bird was able to fly.

"I know that there are lighter than air balloons but they are so limited in maneuverability. I just believe man should be able to fly with the ability of the bird if he could just build the right machine. I built some wings that I strapped to my arms, but I don't have the strength or speed that a bird does in comparison to size. I jumped off the roof of the barn thinking my wings might work, but all I did was shatter my leg when I hit the ground."

Much of his theory was correct to a point so I tried to smooth out the rough areas without being too explicit. I placed one of his stuffed birds on the end of a round, small tree limb so I could show him the necessity of weight and balance. I then pointed out to him the general overall design of the bird, especially the wings that had a thick leading edge that tapered to a thin trailing edge. I also drew a picture for him of the air flow over the wing that caused a low pressure area above and a high pressure area below the wing.

His eyes were aglow with excitement as he took me and showed me a contraption that he believed might fly. This one had wheels on it to roll down a hill in which he might gain enough speed to lift off the ground. As we stood looking at his machine, though he soon realized that his own weight would throw it off balance.

I had so wanted to tell him about my hang glider, but I refrained myself of that.

Soon he turned to me with a look of sheer determination.

"Someday, sir, I will fly. I will."

"I'm sure you will." I answered.

The next morning I asked my hosts where I might purchase a good riding horse for I believed it was time for me to head home.

To perhaps relieve myself of some of the conflict that was raging all around, I dressed myself once again in my buckskins. My hosts of the night before had, at first, been rather dubious thinking at first that I might have been a northern spy. But I left in good standing with them understanding that I was from the Oregon Territory.

CHAPTER EIGHT

I topped a small knoll near the Mississippi River and the scene before me in the draw, brought tension throughout my whole body. There was a man on a horse under a tree limb that I immediately recognized as Ted Hartly. Around Ted's neck was a hanging noose. Colonel Strickland stood at the rear of the horse with his hat pulled low over his beady bloodshot eyes as usual. Just as his hand raised in the air to slap the horse, once again my knife left its scabbard with lightning speed. The knife sliced the rope and stuck in the tree trunk. The timing had been accurate to the point that Ted was jerked from his horse, but fell to the ground making the noose only slightly effective. Colonel Strickland was quick to pull his gun, but upon recognizing me, remembered the barn incident and changed his mind.

"Your frontier garb does not fool me at all. I know you're a spy and I will bring you to justice also. You have interfered with the due process of the law."

It became immediately obvious that the colonel had been imbibing and was somewhat intoxicated. I stopped to check on the condition of Ted as I spoke with the colonel.

"You spoke of the due process of the law. The law, sir offers each individual a trial by an unbiased jury. The only evidence I see before me is an over-zealous colonel, that at this time is under the influence of strong drink. I believe you have tried to take the law into your own hands. Your duties should be engaged with a war that is in process not in a personal endeavor as a bounty hunter."

I disarmed the colonel except for a derringer that was strongly evident in his boot.

"You also speak of me as a spy, Colonel," I added. "Perhaps you're convinced of that, but right now I'm convinced that you have deserted your own command. If it becomes necessary I will deter my trip home to the Oregon Territory to look into the fact of what you are running from. I believe you soothe your own guilt by pursuing Ted."

With that the Colonel quickly mounted and rode off without another word.

"Colonel Strickland is not a colonel. He is a lieutenant that led a company of men to a slaughter. He stole the Colonel's uniform. I know about him and that is why he trails me. I don't know why you are trailing me. I suppose I should be grateful for the rescue, but I'm not wanting company, nor do I need your advice on how to live my life."

With that Ted Hartly also mounted and rode away.

I truly believe that I had been faced with emotional problems that had been brought on by war injuries that could not be treated by pharmacy medicine or healing aided by sutures. I was sure that our paths would cross again and perhaps under more severe circumstances. I was sure that there was much of Colonel Strickland's case that I was unaware of and therefore was intrigued to find out more. Colonel Strickland's course was not hard to follow. The route which the colonel took though was leading back into Union held territory and I couldn't understand why a confederate officer would be placing himself in such jeopardy. The answer to my questions were to be quickly answered. Because of the foliage along the road we traveled, it was easy to stay close to the colonel without being detected. I was soon detected, though, as a company of Union officers soon surrounded both the colonel and myself. I was ordered at gunpoint, off of my horse and taken to stand next to Colonel Strickland. The colonel, though speechless, was obviously surprised by my presence.

An officer soon came to stand face to face with me.

"State your business, sir," he ordered.

"I have had a couple of unsavory run-ins with Colonel Strickland. That has caused me to question his authority. Therefore I have been trailing him."

"Union or Rebel?" came the next question.

"Neither, as a matter of fact, sir. I'm originally from the Oregon Territory. I came to New York and got involved with a doctor from Kentucky. I have been seeking an education that seems of most importance in the territory. I was on my way back home when this situation arose."

My answers seem to be satisfactory for the time being. Colonel Strickland was shackled and I was heavily guarded as we were moved on to a Union command center. At The center Colonel Strickland and I were ushered in to stand before a general's desk. The officer in charge of the abduction filled the general in on the information he had obtained. The general then turned his attention to Colonel Strickland.

"You have been trailed and watched since you defected from the Union Army as a first lieutenant. I have a summary of your maneuvers since that time. I must say, you have been rather destructive to the Confederates whether by chance or choice, I'm not sure. You were given an assignment to the Indian Territory at such time you defected. Why did you defect? Why does Ted Hartly take your concentrated efforts and why do you now ride back into Union Territory? I demand answers."

Orville Strickland stood with a look of confidence, smiling and nodding at times as the general set his case.

"The Lord has been with me in his work. I have not been insubordinate with your authority, sire, just directed by a higher clearer power and the results will attest to that. I was in my tent preparing to go to the Indian Territory. When the voice of the Lord spoke to me of a plan that would bring victory to the Union Army. You, sir, have been decorated with that victory. I would not deny you of that privilege sir and prefer to stay in the background. Ted Hartly is an enemy of the Lord's work that I tried to eliminate. In that case I have failed and I do humbly apologize."

Tears welled up in the colonel's eyes and he choked as if trying to regain his composure. He then straightened himself with confidence again.

"Yet in my failure, sir, the Lord has surely spoken to me again, and I am led to the Indian Territory where I will see great victory."

With the colonel's grand finale, I almost expected to hear a great drum roll or at least a trumpet blast as the curtains fell.

With the inquiry over, I was issued a tent to abide in while a court martial proceeded. I was ordered not to leave whereas I might need to be questioned. At one point I was questioned about my age and abilities, but again the conclusion was that my age by years had to be less than my appearance depicted.

I was not allowed to attend the court martial, but was called in as their final decision was made. Orville Strickland was to retain the rank of colonel and was to leave immediately to help control the Indian uprising in the Colorado area. I was to accompany the colonel and a small wagon train to that territory and then I would be free to again return to Oregon.

Colonel Strickland's nature and conduct had been questionable from the beginning of his military involvement. Sending him to Colorado would cast his personal problems on someone else's shoulders and clear the General's mind to deal with the problems he faced in a raging Civil War. The General said he was counting on me to make sure that Strickland was out of his hair. The governor of the Colorado Territory had requested the help of Colonel Strickland in controlling the Indian problem as he had been a personal friend.

There certainly were some questions I would have liked to ask and some advice I would like to have given, but it would have been most inappropriate at the time. Orville Strickland was a full-fledged colonel and it must have been confirmed in his mind, that which he believed was the voice of the Lord.

Time was quickly moving on and winter's harsh weather in the mountains would soon be approaching our destination, though which was too the settlements along the Platte River. So we calculated our time of arrival to be ahead of the severely foul weather. My own personal idea was to probably winter in the area before moving on to home. Perhaps other delays would stand in my way, but nothing but my own desire pulled me in that direction.

My time with the wagon train gave me an opportunity to reflect more on my time in a foggy state of mind. I was putting most of the picture together, but how much time had elapsed up to my awakening I really wasn't sure. Of course what had really happened on the day of the yellow glow I could only take assumption of. I had always referred to it as the day of the yellow glow in my mind, but I really wasn't sure but what it had much more of a time expanse.

Colonel Strickland took a self-appointed command of the wagon train to the frustration of the man who was actually the wagon master. The colonel took great pains to convince himself that I did not exist. I did not have a wagon, but tried to help those who would have trouble from time to time. The wagon master sought my advice many times as he was sure I must be far more knowledgeable than he. The wagon master's route was designed to avoid hostile Indian encounters as much as possible. Scouts were used so as to give advanced warnings of such possibilities. The train consisted of only ten wagons and therefore the number of men capable of handling firearms was limited. Colonel Strickland studied charts and maps and had tried to enforce different routing that would take the train through known hostile Indian Territory.

"The Lord has directed me to kill Indians and that I will do with hell to pay for anyone who tries to stop me."

For several days it became apparent that a party of about forty Indians were in surveillance of the train. At night precautions were taken and sentry and guard duty assigned. One morning at dawn the Indians were arrayed in battle attire just out of rifle range of the camp. Camp was not broken, but stayed in readiness for several hours. After a while the Indians just turned and rode away. The scouts reported that they had truly left the area, so we broke camp and began to move again. It was obvious to me that our route took us around Indian held territory and therefore, although prepared for hostilities, we were not bent on open confrontation with the Indians, so they left us alone. Colonel Strickland had not been outside of his wagon until the evening after the war party had left. It was at the evening meal that the colonel approached the wagon master and myself and heavily berated us for not opening fire and massacring the Indian. The wagon master was silent while expressions of anger swept his face. I, although, spoke with one comment. "Our actions probably saved your cowardly butt from destruction."

With that the colonel departed again to his wagon and was rarely seen the rest of the journey.

The territorial governor, in the meantime, was busy forming a regiment of men to fight Indians and to be under the command of Colonel Strickland. The regiment was easily formed from men who preferred the Indian wars to being sent south to fight the Confederate Army who had more advanced weaponry.

Fort Lyons, Colorado was a hub-bub of mixed emotion concerning the Indian problem. A local merchant and original settler had married an Indian girl and therefore had two half-breed sons that turned more to their Indian heritage. The situation was a near repeat of the two sons of White Cloud. The commander of Fort Lyons was being replaced as he was judged too sympathetic with the Indians. I was sure that if his policies had gone undisturbed, there surely would have been continued peaceful coexistence, but on the other hand Colonel Strickland had come to the area joining an endeavor with the territorial governor for the main purpose of eliminating the Indians.

In November of that year I stood near the parade grounds as Colonel Strickland worked his troops into an emotional lather. They would be going to the killing fields where no Indians regardless of age or sex would live. The question was put to Colonel Strickland concerning the children. Colonel Strickland entered into an oration stating that they were dealing with non-human savages that must be eliminated from all the earth. "Nits grow into Lice." was his evaluation. All the time while he spoke liquor was being passed around freely. I had started to intervene, but Colonel Strickland seeing me approach ordered me to be bound and removed from the area. His orders were that if I should show any resistance that I should be immediately killed as I was being used by the devil to hamper the true work of God. Four soldiers escorted me about five miles from the fort then let me go and apologized for having to obey the orders of their commanding officer.

I found out that the Indians felt confident of safety for they had been told that if they displayed the American flag no troops would fire on them. Shortly after I had been removed from the parade grounds. An Army captain and a lieutenant broached the subject of peace treaties already activated and the calamity that would follow the breaking of those treaties. Answering vehemently, Colonel Strickland hollered, "By God's command I am here to kill Indians and he who stands in my way will have hell to pay."

My mind, once again began to pour through my acquired information. Once again I asked the question as to why I had been chosen to travel through a repeating history. Was I supposed to solely stop the destruction I so clearly saw forthcoming? I got back to the fort shortly after Colonel Strickland and his regiment left for a place called Sand Creek. How could I as one individual stop a regiment of seven hundred inebriated soldiers? Could I outride them and warn the Indians? The Indians already believed they were safe. Could one lone man convince them otherwise? It seemed impossible for me to change the tide of events, but my mind was a tangle of turmoil, question and guilt. I was able to talk to the officer that had been replaced and his emotions were torn like mine. Our hands were tied so we were hopeless to change the course of calamity that was about to occur.

It was the following afternoon that Colonel Strickland and his troops rode back into the fort. The colonel rode straight and proud, but his troops looked sick and discouraged. At his report Colonel Strickland said that four to six hundred braves had been killed and gave a glowing report that only twenty-eight soldiers had been killed. During his report a lieutenant stood to his feet, weeping and obviously heart-sickened.

"There were only maybe thirty braves in the whole camp. The rest were on a hunting expedition. Those killed or should I say slaughtered were women and children. I was standing near a dying pregnant Indian lady when the colonel ordered me to cut child from her and remove its intestines." At that the lieutenant literally got sick and had trouble containing himself to continue. "You might court martial me, or even hang me, but I will never be involved in a slaughter like that again."

At that the lieutenant stripped his army jacket of all insignia and began to leave. The major post commander went to his side and spoke loudly for all to hear.

"I will conduct a thorough investigation." Colonel Strickland did a sharp military "about face" and was obviously angry and started to protest, but the major interrupted him. "If, Colonel, you did indeed conduct your campaign in honor as you say, then you have nothing to worry about, but there will be an investigation. It is obvious that some of your troops don't feel as victorious as you, that in conjunction with the inebriation I saw when you left requires an investigation."

The next day I was asked to ride with a number of others to the Sand Creek area. With the number was the man who was the father of two half-breed braves that had been at Sand Creek at the time of the attack. As we rode into the Sand Creek sight, Mr. Bennet rode in front of us so that if the braves were back in camp, they would know we had not come for more destruction. The Bennet brothers were there with several others of the tribe as we did our investigation of the obvious carnage and slaughter all around us.

Mr. Bennet cried as he tried to apologize to his sons for the injustice that was done and explained that the major with which the peace treaty had been made, had been replaced mainly by the governor who had also called in Colonel Strickland.

The Bennet brothers surely reminded me of the Cloud brothers of long ago. One seemed to have a more forgiving and understanding spirit about him, although his heart was obviously pained with the great loss around him. They both were silent as their father spoke and then the more aggressive brother answered. "I respect you for you are my father, but you are white. I therefore by blood am half white. If I could use my knife to drain half my blood to become all Indian, I would do that here before you. If I see you in battle I will not kill you. You will kill me before I kill you. You stand alone as a white man. No one else stands with you. I will gather all Indians together, friend and foe, and we will destroy all crazy whites like Colonel Strickland. We will not listen to peace treaty lies. I will persuade my mother to come back to her people. If the white man stands, he will stand alone."

Mr. Bennet was too heart sick to even answer his son.

As Mr. Bennet sat in silence and sorrow, I spoke up relating my knowledge of Colonel Strickland and asked if I would have been effective as a lone rider had I come to warn them. My question was not answered, but the silence spoke that while I was with his white father I would be given safety out of the camp, but after that I was a fair kill. As yet I have not been able to satisfy my mind with what should have been done and that perhaps I had somewhat failed in the mission that my existence was called to accomplish.

Although I truly believed that Orville Strickland was possessed of some morbid spirit for sure, he was never rightfully made to stand accountable for his treachery. Mr. Bennet was put to blame more than Colonel Strickland. Several of the soldiers that had been at Sand Creek were privately discharged or turned up missing. The older Bennet brother was found in a remote area, having been tortured and hanged. The younger brother was captured and sentenced to prison in Yuma, Arizona. The whole incident, although split through the middle in the attitude of the people, soon became a subject not to be discussed for fear of greater conflict.

I had tried to be of some comfort to the prematurely aging Mr. Bennet, but it was all too obvious that he did indeed stand alone.

Although not identical by any means, the situation was so close in comparison to the Cloud family, that my heart was moved with such empathy as to be almost unbearable. Had white men been more prevalent at the time of the Cloud family? It might have been even closer in similarity. I could not imagine Desert Flower leaving White Cloud to go back to her own people and the thought of his sons being there when Desert Flower's spirit left was comforting indeed. I remembered Summer Cloud coming to seek the wisdom of White Cloud and wondered what the future held for Mr. Bennet. Would there even be a peaceful coexistence between people of different heritage and skin color? What about religious preference that I had come aware of, like the Methodist or the Holiness? Yes, the modern times that I had known had its problems and perhaps they were the magnified problems of this age that I found myself in.

You are correct in that I have let my mind wonder again. Questions come to my mind that I don't have the answers for, even though I have been able to observe so much. I don't understand whether it is a blessing or a curse, but when problems become too great, I have been removed from them. Prior to the day of the yellow glow life had seemed to be too complicated and I had longed for a more simple life. At the passing of Desert Flower I had left the area for a lengthy period of time, now here in Colorado was a situation that had become overbearing to me and I was on my way to the Arizona Territory.

The countryside was heavy with winter, so I knew a northern route home would be difficult. It had still been in my mind that maybe I could be of some help to the younger Bennet brother, but he too had been murdered before his departure was underway.

My travel was very similar to that as it had been many other times. I traveled alone with a riding horse and one pack horse. Some of the gear that I had acquired was rather different than that of earlier years. Yes, I still lived off the land for my sustenance. Whenever I killed a deer, bear or cougar there was no waste and much of the beast would travel on with me this time, though, I felt it a necessity to be better armed with weaponry, so I carried with me a Spencer repeating rifle and two model 1860, 44 caliber bolt guns, plus a good supply of ammo/ I had not forgotten the attitude of the territory's Indians as was expressed by the older Bennet brother. I had also overheard a statement by Colonel Strickland that expressed that his desire was far from being dilatory in seeing my end come about. It was these very things that had caused me to be very cautious and observant. It was also this observation that had led me to realize that for three days I had been followed. The distance of the followers made it next to impossible to know if it was one follower or more. It had become clear in my mind that I must come up with some stratagem that would put me to the greater advantage. The countryside I traveled through was mostly open and meeting with other people was rare. I seemed to be entering into an area that was hillier and with greater amounts of vegetation. I understood that in a more dense area my own observation of my pursuers would be limited and that a surprise attack could be more feasible. I had been traveling in a south westerly direction and was getting in closer proximity with a stream. I figured that I would eventually cross the stream, but if I followed it more closely I might be able to find an area where a diversion was more probable. I angled my route to the stream in such a way that it would appear that my route would be more southerly. I followed a wide shallow part of the stream for some distance. When I first came in contact with the stream I had noticed that at a distance to the north it merged with another stream that came from a more mountainous area. When I finally entered the stream I turned back north and hot-tailed it to the merging stream that came from due west. I rode up that stream to a southerly knoll that was heavy with trees and brush but afforded a good view far to the south and a ways to the north. It was there that I set up a concealed camp for however long I might have to stay. As I was to later find out, those trailing me had also been observant of the terrain and seeing me alter the course had decided to close the gap quickly. I had left my camp and had taken a hideout near the creek edge. It was only a short time 'til two riders came above the edge of the creek not ten feet from me. I recognized the two as some of then that had been in close proximity to Colonel Strickland almost constantly. They quickly saw my tracks and turned down the bed of the stream to find where I might have exited. They hadn't gone very far when I heard a noise behind me, but before I had a chance to examine there was a dark skinned arm about my neck with a razor sharp blade against my throat. Almost immediately a shot rang out near my ear and I was quickly disarmed. As the other two riders came back I was marched to the edge of the stream.

"Good work, Chief. Now I want you to disrobe him, not clear naked, but I want nothing hidden in those buckskins. Colonel said he was a cagey one and not to be trusted."

As soon as I was stripped of all my outer clothing they told the Indian scout that he was dismissed of duty and could go back to the fort and be handsomely paid. Before the Indian had gone twenty feet the sergeant shot him in the back of the head.

"There's your pay in lead, dog dead Indian." He then roared in laughter. All the while the corporal was tying a hangman's noose the sergeant was holding my trial, himself being the judge and jury.

"You have been a naughty, naughty boy. What with insubordination with the colonel and openly standing in the way of justice, you have now lied to the people saying you were headin' to the Oregon Territory. This isn't the way to Oregon, so you must be punished. You will be hanged, shot and then burned. There is no escape for you so pray hard stranger." With that the sergeant again laughed. He had gotten off his horse and was approaching me to tie me up when a close proximity shot rang out and a hole appeared just above the sergeant's left ear. The sergeant slumped and fell into me knocking me off my feet. The corporal turned quickly to make a get away, but two more shots rang out. One shot hit the corporal in the left kidney area and the other in the back of his left arm, but he kept going hard. I rolled over staying behind the sergeant's body to see Ted Hartly near where my hideout was, a smoking pistol in his hand.

"We're even now, Doc. So you can head on to the Oregon Territory, but you are going the wrong direction."

"I am much obliged, Ted." I answered

"But northern travel in the winter has not appealed to me and about due west of here is a vast maze of almost impassable canyons. I had planned on going a little more southward than west through the Arizona Territory to California and then north." Are you still heading to California to be with your sisters?"

I was thankful for the fact that there was still some trace of humane feelings in Ted's personality. Perhaps the actions in my defense was the last strain of it that would appear for I saw a hard steel coldness in his once youthful, naive and caring eyes.

"Headin' to Texas. I have now killed ten men and I'm not welcome amongst decent folk. By the time you get to your weapons I'll be gone. I hope I never see you again, cause if I do you'll be an enemy and I'll have to kill you. You are traveling through dangerous Apache and outlaw territory so I probably won't have to do that."

I don't remember if I closed my eyes for a second or looked away, but when I looked back Ted was gone.

I stripped the sergeant and the Indian of their weaponry and took their horses along with me. Perhaps I would use them for trade.

The day was far spent, but the events of that day were too intense for me to let an idle mind deal with, so I traveled through the night and all the next day.

Santa Fe was a small town in size but very large in activity as Independence. It seemed to be a town of great wagon train activity. Along with this it was part of a cattle drive trail and of military activity trying to control the Spanish, Navajo and Apache uprisings. It had at first been controlled by the Confederates, but then taken over by the Union. Santa Fe was really too far out of contact with Civil War activities to be of vast importance. Without a doubt it also possessed its share of saloons and brothels. I had stayed in Santa Fe three months in which time I had become acquainted with a wagon master that was putting together a train to take the route of the Spanish Trail. Most of the occupants of the trail were of the Mormon sect and were heading to Salt Lake.

The government had sent troops into this territory in the year of fifty-seven to try and stamp them out due to their act of polygamy at which time they said that they had abandoned that practice. I surely didn't want to cause a ruckus by exposing them, but it was rather strange to me to see a wagon with one man, two or three women and several children. One man, when questioned about it, said that two of the women with him were widows due to the martyrdom they had dealt with in Illinois. Time and age didn't seem to add up properly to me, but I realized that freedom of religion was an issue that was probably more intense then than what it was in the modernistic world I had lived in. I knew that in the time that I had lived in before the yellow flash there had been a couple of different fellows that claimed to be great prophets like the Mormon leader had, but led their people to destruction in one of the cases. The military and law enforcement had been involved and the repercussions from that incident rolled on in magnitude causing great disaster for some time. Persecution and force against an unwanted sedition seems only to bring out the intrinsic value in the believers involved. The crucifying of the God man, Jesus in the Bible surely did not put a stop to his teaching. It only enhanced it and gave it strength.

Oh my! I have left my narrative again, but you see it had been so strong on my mind to question the reason for my existence. Did I need to act in such a way as to change the cause of history? Had I failed at Sand Creek? How could I stop the effects of the war as exemplified in Ted Hartly? Perhaps alone we cannot change everything, but that does not give us the right to turn our backs. We must do something!

The route of the train would surely put us into more mountainous areas so I was in no hurry and waited patiently for a more aesthetic period. In my waiting time I was thrust into another situation wherein the clarity of the reason for my existence again was brought to light. As I said before, we have no right to turn away from the negative situation if we have any knowledge at all of how to bring about a better result. Perhaps I had been wrong in running from Sand Creek, but I had been at a total loss of which action to take or to have taken to being about a better finale. To that which I am about to relate, I knew what I must do, but was threatened rather vehemently.

I had been involved with the wagon master repairing wagons and making sure everything was in order. The staging area was very near the corrals or stockyard area. I had not paid close attention to that area until a gun battle broke out. Right in the middle of it was none other than Ted Hartly. He was with a couple others holding off several other men including the sheriff. I was about to try and intervene when Ted took a slug in the chest. The other men with him were quickly brought down, one with a slug over his right eye and the other with a close proximity shotgun blast that left him with only an open cavity for a chest. I ran to Ted and found him still alive and gasping. A young boy was nearby and I tossed him a twenty dollar gold piece and told him where my bag was and to bring it quickly. I had started cutting away the clothing from Ted's chest when the sheriff put a gun to the back of my head.

"Get away from him. He's wanted dead or alive. Preferably dead. He's my prisoner either way." "And, sir, you will probably have him the way you prefer, but I'm not your enemy so get your gun off my neck."

Another man stepped up whom I didn't recognize, but who obviously knew me.

"Sheriff the man that you are talking with is a multi-talented man, not only is he a doctor, but he is quick as lightning with a knife and body. I swear that if you even begin to bring that hammer back you'll exchange places with him before you know it and have his knife at your throat." The sheriff took his gun away, but continued his discourse of Ted being prisoner. The boy had returned with my bag and I first brought out the ether solution that the Indians called sleeping water. I moistened a piece of Ted's shirt and placed it over his mouth and nose. By this time quite a crowd had gathered and the sheriff was detained from trying to reprimand me to trying to control the crowd. Someone had brought a blanket and I placed Ted on it, but knew I would move him no farther. With extensive surgery and a great loss of blood I knew Ted's chances of survival was almost nil. The fact of unsanitary conditions also was a negative, but I knew I must try. Several times I asked for some piece of equipment to use and it would appear almost immediately. When I split Ted's breast bone and separated it to reveal a slowly beating heart, I couldn't help but hear the gasps of shock expressed by onlookers.

The slug had passed through the outer sac of the heart barely missing the heart itself. It had lodged in Ted's spine and I knew he would be paralyzed waist down if he did in fact live. Other damage, though, was minimal. It had been mid-morning when the shooting occurred, but it had started getting dark by the time I made my final closure. At that time I had plenty of help to move Ted to a hotel room where I would be with him for a month and long after the wagon train had left.

When Ted finally regained consciousness to the point of being alert to his condition and surroundings his emotions broke.

"I was dying, Doc and I saw the other side. I would have died too, but an angel stepped up and told the sheriff to leave you alone so you could fix me. You got to believe me, Doc. I was going to Hell if it hadn't been for you and that angel. I might die in prison, but I won't go to Hell now."

Ted's emotions broke so violently that I had to sedate him again. The next time that Ted regained consciousness, a Texas Ranger and the sheriff were his visitors, I reported Ted's condition and his future as a paralytic. I also told them of the physiological trauma that had taken place in Ted's life brought on by the war and his near death experience. There was an extensive discussion that took place in which the sheriff wanted to without further ado, take Ted out and hang him. After some time the Texas Ranger told the sheriff to dig a grave and bury a dog or whatever in it and put Ted Hartly's name on the tombstone.

"I am going to report that Ted Hartly was shot and killed. The man that I'm looking at now will not be Ted Hartly. He will no longer appear in these parts. Doc, take him to Oregon with you or do something with him away from this territory. Ted Hartly is dead?"

Before the ranger left I made it clear that I wanted to be left alone when I left with Ted. I didn't want the sheriff or some other bounty hunter plaguing me.

Just about a week before I was to leave with Ted, or who was now known as Billy Armstrong, a beautiful Indian lady came to our room. I had a rather difficult time putting a restraint on my own emotions for the lady's features, although more (may I say heavenly) were very much in likeness to the young Desert Flower.

"You will have nothing to worry about on your journey with Billy Armstrong for my people and I will be your guardians. You will not see us, but we will be nearby and on constant watch out. We will herd good game your way when needed."

"You will take Billy north past the Great Salt Lake near Montana Territory to a place of many boiling water. There Billy will stay and bathe in many mineral waters and get well and walk again"

I had not wanted her to go but soon she was gone and my emotions all a wack except for the strong sense that this time I had done the right thing, although probably not by myself or by my own merit.

I will say not much about my trip to the place of boiling waters or known in the other times as Yellowstone. I had prepared a special wagon for Ted, whoops I mean Billy and I had also been somewhat successful in designing a brace that allowed him minimal movement of his lower extremities. Perhaps I would have had no reason to fear, but for the sake of caution, I kept all weaponry out of sight or on my own person. Billy had become almost a religious fanatic I might say. Maybe more bad men should see the other side and visions of Hell. That is not within my realm to create such visions though. I have always believed that there certainly were creations being made to minister or to guard and protect the human being, although perhaps I have never seen them. That is unless the Indian lady as such. I do know that she was most as assuredly within the realm of the aesthetic. Billy, on the other hand, becomes a worshiper of angels for they had been manifested to him. I had tried to discuss the fact that God himself was to be worshipped and that also was the job of angels, but his fanaticism was strong and at least it was better than being a gun-slinging killer.

Well, we did reach the land of boiling water and there I set Billy up with a cabin and the means to sustain himself. When I offered him a rifle to hunt with, he very quickly refused and said he would never again have the need for weaponry. Years later I heard of a man named Billy Armstrong. A strong, healthy, very religious man that made his abode near and about Yellowstone.

CHAPTER NINE

When I finally rode out of the Yellowstone area my mind was at a loss for direction. In Billy Armstrong's opinion (which I could not change) I was probably heading back to Heaven where angels took their abode while awaiting a new assignment. I could only look back at my acquaintances with Shebbard Douglas and the Sand Creek ordeal to see two major failures. We so often torture ourselves with the what ifs and the if only. For some reason unbeknownst to me, I had been given a second chance. Other than a few medical mercies and the direction I had given Kavwan, I believed I had at the most part missed the point. The cloud family existence should have created a peaceful coexistence between the red man and white man. Mr. Bennet at Fort Lyons was in a similar situation as White Cloud had been, but Mr. Bennet had been so devastated and the red man - white man conflict had been escalated beyond comprehension.

Perhaps I should have headed west, back to the Oregon Territory and once again lost myself in the security of the canyons, but I had also had a compelling urge to rectify the Sand Creek situation. So here I was again, torn between running away from the problem or sticking my nose back into the escalating unchangeable results of a failure.

For a number of years I had wandered around in the area of the Sioux Nation. I had sat in counsel with the Indian braves and chiefs, although never molested. I had learned about a man from the far south that was preaching the unity of all Indian tribes. Trying to gather them into one unit. This idea had come to fruition with the Sioux and they stood as a mighty nation.

Wovoka's message to the Indian was that the dead would all return one day. The buffalo would be restored and the Indian would stand as one mighty nation. This message that the Messiah will one day return to gather his children in a land of bliss with no death, sorrow or tears.

It seemed strange to me that as I sit in these council meetings in a smoky dim lit atmosphere, I would catch a glimpse of the Indian lady that had entered my room in Santa Fe. Sometimes the man that approached as the sheriff had his gun to the back of my head, would be with her. When I would see them, thoughts would race through my mind with questions I could not answer. Were they still protecting me? How long had they been watching over me? If I had had the ability to enter the spirit world as White Cloud's people believed or if I was a heavenly ambassador as Billy Armstrong was convinced of, then I surely would have been able to communicate with these two openly and would not have to seek direction. No, although there was much of my existence that I did not understand, I did indeed understand that I was far from being angelic or heavenly. Whatever my existence was, the Indians respected me as a man of great wisdom and listened to my council. Several times some of the young braves, seeing my skin to be white, wanted to eliminate me, but the chiefs would soon still them. It was under such conditions that I was able to set in council with the Sioux war chief himself. It had been said of him that he was good to listen to and sometimes bad not to. On this one occasion he seemed to want to listen to what I had to say.

"Not very many moons away and you will have a great victory, but soon the great victories will be no more and you will be forced to leave behind the life you have known."

"The white man has destroyed the buffalo to take away the strength of the red man. Those who seek the wisdom of Wankan Tonka will survive. Those who seek their own strength and wisdom will die."

"It is a good thing that the red man seeks unity but he should have sought it long ago. Then the white man would not have been strong enough. A lodge divided against itself will fall."

"I have taken counsel about you for a long time. I have learned that you take counsel in the spirit world and I believe what I have been told. It is too late for all tribes to unite. Some will not even though it means defeat. The Crow remains our enemy. The white man destroys our livelihood by killing the buffalo. He steals our land, puts us on reservations that will not sustain us. They try to tell us about their God, but to me there is but one God, WankanTonka."

"Now I must fight to defend my people, the old man and the young. I am tired of fighting, of blood and loss of our braves. If I die in battle, it is more honorable, but to lay down and peacefully give up our land and bow to a strange God, I will not."

"I long for the old days and our way of life. If that is gone then it is a good day to die."

I knew I had talked to another great man in history. He knew what was sacred to him. His beloved older sister's family had been massacred by the Crow and although his sister had escaped, he now believed her to be dead and his vengeance on the Crow was bitter indeed.

It surprised me that he had mentioned myself taking counsel in the spirit world. Did the existence of White Cloud still invade Indian counsel, or was the presence of the Indian lady that I had encountered at Santa Fe actually been the lingering spirit of Desert Flower? These were questions I could not answer.

At Sand Creek I have somehow failed to warn the Indians of coming destruction. Maybe I should warn the white general this time of coming destruction, but on the other hand I see the near future battle and outcome as a scent of payback for the injustice at Sand Creek.

The General, although probably as cocky and bullheaded as Colonel Strickland, I'm sure wasn't as inhumane in nature. I was also sure that getting an audience with him would be useless as well as next to impossible.

My heart ached as I saw the coming defeat of a once noble people and the depressing aftermath it would leave. I thought of the Cloud family and how peaceful those years had been and it brought about once more the longing to be home, however the question of my purpose for being chosen for the task before me was still heavy on my mind. If the lady in my foggy state of mind was still alive and in the New York area, then I must again try and contact her. If I could remember a name, it would give me a greater advantage. Well, New York was a long ways away so perhaps something would stir my mind to remembrance.

Here I go again and you'll have to excuse me for yet another little detour from my narrative, as I prepared to head back to New York and squelch the idea of heading home, the first impression that came to my mind was, "This will probably delay me another several years. To my nearest calculation it had been twenty-seven years since I had left the cove and had gone with Shebbard Douglass, I got rather nostalgic thinking that by now Shebbard was an elderly statesman. What if it were another twenty-five or thirty years before I got back home? If I was fifty years old on the day of the yellow glow then I would be almost eighty by the time I get back. Oh my goodness, if my awakening had been in 1690 and I was fifty, then at this point I would be two hundred and thirty-six years old, and besides that how many years had I been in a foggy state of mind? My, my, oh my. Well anyway my conclusion was that I guess time and aging just wasn't supposed to be a concern of mine. Unbelievable? I really don't blame you, but read on. It might at least be interesting. Don't you think?! When the Biblical Noah began to build his huge craft and told people that it was going to rain and flood the whole earth, well if they would have had mental asylums at that time, ol' Noah would have ended up having a permanent care home. The earth being covered by a mist, they didn't know what rain was and had probably never seen a clear sky. Well, anyway, if I was not the only survivor of the yellow glow day then I must communicate with others of like experience and that would mean clearing away more of the fog that existed up until my awakening.

Concerning the lady I had been with I recalled that we both were of German descent and both knew we had had a common experience that had caused us to be (shall I say different). In recollection of my supposed dream we had been together five hundred years and had borne many children. Had she therefore taken my name and would she still go by that name. My German name would be Wilhelm with the "W" being pronounced "V". I understood that in the other time many of the Scandanavian people had settled in Minnesota and then migrated from there to the Dakotas, so my route would be the same, in reverse. The Dakotas were only sparsely settled as yet in this time, so Minnesota would be my best bet and my story would be that I was seeking my own heritage. Another thought began rolling through my mind that rather intrigued me. My great grandmother had come from Germany, bound for Wisconsin. They had been in Minnesota where my grandfather was born just shortly after their arrival in America. When my Grandpa was approximately ten years old they had moved to North Dakota and then due to the weather in 1888 they moved to the Spokane, Washington area. There had been a bad blizzard with temperatures at minus 40°C the winter of 1888-89. I had camped on the Powder River as these thoughts began racing through my mind. Was I then going to be looking for my own Grandpa who I would be much older than? In the other time there had been a song written, "I'm my own Grandpa". One line, repeated several times was, "It's funny I know, but it really is so, I'm my own Grandpa."

I soon found myself hysterically laughing so hard I couldn't even stand up. My, in Indian vs. white hostile area, one should be rather quiet, but in this scenario I was not quiet at all. I soon became fully aware that a white and an Indian man were both in real close with weapons drawn and aimed my direction.

"You must be scouts for Auntie."

"That we are," they replied. "And who might you be?"

"Well, I'm just a traveler, but one that might be able to give you warning." "Do you happen to be Mich and Curly?" Curly as a Crow Indian scout that had he been a woman, could have been considered rather pretty. They both put away their weapons and looked at me almost unbelieving

"How do you know us and who are you?" I was wondering about their question myself, again wondering if my knowledge came recently or from the other time.

"I'm one whom you will never see again, but I warn you that you face great defeat. Curly, you will be an only survivor. You and the horse named Comanche."

Mich spoke after a while. "We have observed the Sioux village and it is mostly women and children. I believe you to be mad (whoever you are). Or perhaps you are a spy for the Sioux."

"If in fact you have observed a solitary Indian village, did you not question where the braves might be? One obscure village doesn't represent the whole Sioux nation. Your Seventh Cavalry might question the whereabouts of Crazy Horse. I'm sure you have considered more than one village. I'm here to warn you of coming disaster. If you heed that warning or not is up to you. I say no more."

I had done my part sharing my observation with both the Indian and the Calvary. Did I, in this, sooth my own conscience? I still questioned, what more I could have done. It kind of reminded me of the Old Testament prophets that warned Israel of coming exile to Babylon. Some listened, most didn't.

I'm sure that the encounter brought questions to their minds that might have even got back to the colonel. Several other warnings and insight had come to him, none of which had much impact on his determined mind.

So it came about that June of 1876 the entire Seventh Cavalry was wiped out by the Sioux nation under the leadership of Chief Crazy Horse. An incident that would not be forgotten throughout history.

I began to think of the element of time. Had I been placed in the future? I might have been able to change the past, whenever I was sent back, but being placed in the past how would it have been possible to change anything? I had been placed in some kind of time warp from which I had gone through an outer space worm hole. However, to have reversed the procedure, to travel into the past, I would have had to have gone through this time warp to an advanced state, in other words into the future and then to be placed back to the exact time of entrance. That theory didn't make sense to me because I had been placed far back in the past which was scientifically impossible. If I were able, somehow to change the past, then the future would also be changed.

I had felt, sort of, guilty concerning Sand Creek, as though I could have somehow stopped the outcome. Maybe I should just be happy that I was successful in turning Ted Hartley's life around.

Again I have let my mind drift off of the narrative, trying to find answers to my many questions. In the other time, space travel was becoming rather common and therefore many questions were asked. For instance, if you boarded a rocket on a certain date and traveled backwards of the rotation of the event at a warped speed, and landed at the same spot several days later, would the date be the same as when you left or would you have reversed time? The thought was that the more intense the gravitational pull the faster time advanced, but how could that be reversed, unless the yellow glow was a time of reversed gravity.

I had been rather pleased with my experience and life, but how this had happened and the reason for it evaded me.

CHAPTER TEN

In North Dakota I did find a German immigrant settlement. Within that settlement was the Wilhelm family that had come from a place called Schneidemuhl. The man's name was Julius and his wife's name was Augusta. Augusta was named after a matron ancestor of the Wilhem family who had lived a very long life and then disappeared, not to be heard from again. They asked me of my heritage and I told them that a lot of my heritage was a mystery to me. Mystery indeed. How could I honestly tell them that I was their great grandchild and also that in the essence of time I was also their many times over great grandfather. Augusta did tell me of a woman that had accosted her when she disembarked in New York, saying that she was the original Augusta and that she had lived eight hundred years or more.

"She troubled me much until I reported her to some authority and the last I knew she had been placed in an asylum." I was glad that I was able to have a command of the German language because neither one of them spoke a lick of English.

Well to say the least this situation was getting rather weird so I proceeded on my journey to New York.

In New York I was finally able to locate a mental hospital that had had a patient named Augusta Wilhem some fifteen years back, but had been released as harmless. I was told that she had come in contact with two other associates and had gone to Kentucky to find another. They called themselves the survivors.

I was troubled with the idea of further pursuit of the survivors. Perhaps they were trying to find me as I had been in Kentucky with Don Brookshire for some time. Well, I decided it surely wouldn't hurt to check on the place I had labored at for a period of time. Perhaps some of the old patience would still be around. Again I bought a set of street clothes and trimmed my beard back. My hair was still long.

I was able to contact some of my old patience, however it was hard for them to accept me for myself as nearly thirty years had passed and I had not noticeably aged.

I heard about a religious group that was headed up by three people that called themselves The Survivors. They claimed to be angels that were sent by God to save the world from destruction. Anti-war, anti-government, anti-establishment, that had a small following for a while. I was told two of them were eventually hung and the third, a woman, had been deported. I broke out into a cold sweat. Colonel Strickland had almost accomplished having me hung. Perhaps I had been fulfilling my mission and purpose. At least enough so as I still survived. I would no longer search for other survivors and I only hoped they would not search for me. Yes, it might answer some questions, but then it might not. I would live my extra time the best that I could, and would not allow myself to be influenced by outside forces. Right now I felt it time to go home. I had been away almost forty years.

The transcontinental railroad had opened sometime in 1869 and that would take me to San Francisco.

I had been in New York for a year and in Kentucky for four years. I had gotten involved with a reconstruction endeavor, and the slavery problem that was far from over. The whites had created a system of legalized depression to try and keep the blacks in their place. That along with the forming of the Ku-Klux-Klan was keeping the heat on the prejudicism and segregation problems. It reminded me of the dilemma that the San Francisco constable faired during the '49 Gold Rush. Many blacks, with education and drive would overcome and make a name for themselves in history. George Washington Carver and Booker T. Washington to name a couple. Many others would succumb to depression. I thought of a black man by the name of Bass Reeves who was making a name for himself as a Lone Texas Ranger.

I had gotten acquainted with a black family that had been rather successful on the little farm they had acquired. The man had invented and built most of his farming equipment. They were wanting to send their two children to school. As I stood in their yard a group of KKK approached. I stood facing them with my weapons fully displayed and was ordered to stand aside.

"My pistols have six shots a piece. That makes 12. My carbine has 5 shots. That makes 17, my knife is unlimited and I don't miss. Now how many of you want to die?"

I later on found a teacher that would school the two children and helped the black man get some of his inventions patented and on the road to be manufactured.

Well, I hadn't solved the whole problem, but at least one family was helped and perhaps that would become infectious to spread to others.

Now as I sat on the train's passenger car enroute to San Francisco I saw a change coming on fast. Roads were being built. Telegraph lines were being set. Steam powered the engine that pulled this train and also now the drive of some big ships. The Indians were being forced to live on reservations. The old ways were fast disappearing and the new was taking over.

In San Francisco I had another choice to make. I could hoof it alone the way I had come, I could take the overland stage most of the way, or I could take a steam ship to Portland.

Although If I choose the later it would almost deplete my available funds, so I decided to hoof it or take the stage when I could. I knew this would take longer, however, I knew my abode in the canyon probably no longer existed, so time wasn't of the essence.

When I was leaving the train depot, I spotted a lumber wagon with a sign on the side which identified it as a wagon from the S.D. & Sons Lumber and Contracting Co. I asked the driver if the S.D. stood for Shebard Douglass. "Indeed it does. They have a couple of large log mills way to the north which supplies lumber to numerous construction companies." He told me that Shebard had passed away two years prior and that his two sons now ran the business. He asked me if I had known Shebard and the circumstances of my acquaintance. I'm sure that if I would have told him the details there would have been doubt and unanswerable questions asked. "Yes, I got acquainted with him sometime back and a finer gentleman would be hard to find."

In Sacramento as I was loading my baggage, the driver mentioned that it looked like I had some weaponry. When I told him I did, he said that his shotgun driver was unavailable and wondered if I would take the job, besides the coach was loaded to capacity. It would take approximately 5 days to get to Northern California near to the Oregon border. They hadn't had much trouble through the flat valley, however over the mountains in the Shasta area there had been frequent robberies. A lot of the lawmen in those days had dabbled on both sides of the law so if a job came available and you were good with a gun you qualified and so it was that I was given a test of my ability as a shooter and was therefore deputized to ride shotgun to be a protector of the stage and its cargo. Most of the gold shipments in the area were toward Frisco so the northbound, away from gold country was usually slim pickings for the highwaymen, however transferring of funds was common.

Among the passengers of this particular run, was a man who owned a big gold mining enterprise and was heading north to invest in a logging expedition. I asked him if he had ever heard of a man named Timothy Lautter. He told me that he had bought Tim Lautter out and he had gone east somewhere to be with his in-laws where his own parents had passed on. "That, sir, was more than thirty years ago. He had told me of a silver-haired mountain man that had saved his life as he was mighty swift and accurate with a knife." He looked at me quickly and then shook his head. "No way possible you could be the same man." The question of my age and existence surfaced again so I just turned and walked away. The incident with Tim Lautter had been thirty-four years prior.

This trip had gone rather smooth, that is as smooth a stage could be, until we were in a gully, crossing a creek near the city of Red Bluff. Around a bend in the road we came to a log and pile of brush across the road. The driver brought the stage to a stop and said, "This don't look good at all." Soon two mounted men with guns drawn approached. "We are only after one man. Cooperate with us and the rest of you can go your way. Now driver and shot, you just toss down your weapons all gentle like then come on down and stand right here." I had a long coat that covered my knife and I was hoping they didn't see it as effective against a gun. As I stood real near the mounted rider the other bandit approached the coach with his gun pointed to the door while demanding passengers to disembark. I saw my time to make my move and as if in one action my knife let my right hand and with my left hand I jerked the mounted rider to the ground. The driver went to take possession of the gun on the ground and I secured the man that was on the ground. Later when I went to bind up a wrist and remove my knife. The business man looked at me with an expression of shock. "You were acquainted with Tim Lautter who told me of a similar circumstance. Coincidence? Maybe, but how old are you anyway?"

"I really don't keep close track of my age. The last I knew about it I was fifty. But, yes, sir, coincidence for sure."

The stage made its final stop in Red Bluff and would head back south the next day. When it stopped it was trailing two horses and two tightly secured prisoners.

The next day as I was to depart the hotel a sheriff approached me and said I was to report to the stage office and he escorted me there.

"Sir, you have been offered two different jobs. Number one, I would like to offer you the job of stage driver. You mightily impressed us for sure."

The sheriff spoke next. "I have sent a number of telegrams and the state of California would like to hire you as a Ranger. I'm sure the pay could be rather lucrative."

"Sirs, I do appreciate the offers, but the last time I actually held a regular job was during the Civil War when I worked as a doctor's assistant."

"My desire at this point is to go into Oregon in search of my heritage."

The sheriff spoke again. "The two men that you almost single handedly captured had a reward over them. You are the recipient of that reward. Besides that, the man that they were after has also left you a substantial reward. Will you be willing to accept those rewards?"

"I will accept the rewards, however I'd rather not be made well-known all over the country which would put me in jeopardy of assailants."

The sheriff laughed. "Sir, it's too late to hide your reputation. Edward Westlake's knowledge of a past similar incident with Tim Lautter, which has tied you in with knowing the late Shebard Douglass. Questions will be asked and answered. Ken Douglass, Shebard's son is now on his fast journey here to meet with you. Oh, and by the way, any assailant that would try to challenge you would be foolish indeed. I plead with you to stay at least another day."

I ended up staying almost four days, much to my displeasure. I believed that the other survivors had brought about their own demise by self-exploitation in political, religious and environment community decisions. When I had exposed myself in an anger fit in front of Sheb, it had immediately caused a change in our relationship. I realized that, in an advancing scientific age, the search for facts would stronger be. Soon the nineteen and two thousand years would be on the world and modern technology would be strong again. Although this was strong in my mind, I wasn't ready yet. I wasn't sure that I had been successful in bringing about the purpose of my (different) existence. The sheriff had said that questions would be asked and answered and that had kept sleep from my eyes.

It was the evening of the second day that Ken Douglass and another man, Brent Holdow arrived. We had an evening meal together where the conversation was light and get acquainted friendly. I found out that Brent Holdow was a history and science professor at a university in Frisco.

At the next day's meeting, Edward Westlake was also there. Ken Douglas was very much in attitude and features as was his father.

Ken began, "I must begin with the fact of the great respect my father had for you and I am sure that if he were here today, he would begin with a sincere apology for the change in his demeanor after the incident on the river. You must admit that what seemed to have been in a road bed with a remnant of asphalt indicating long lost culturistic society. Your reaction and the incurring slide was more than he could handle at that time."

I answered, "The situation mentioned has been an embarrassment to me ever since."

"The beginning of the book of Genesis in the Bible, the words are thus, 'and the earth was void and formless,' some have injected the words, "became void," thus indicating a lost society. I do not add the word, "became." I did see that as a scar though, by who I don't know, and my reactions were wrong."

Brent then took the conversation, "There has been vast evidence of lost societies, such as the Incas of South America. The Roman road was paved. I take it then you don't believe in a lost civilization?"

"Sir, I believe the world was once cleaned by flood and God preserved Noah's family."

Ken spoke again, "Dad was under the assumption that if you weren't a survivor of a lost civilization then you must be an angel in disguise. Age does not seem to affect you."

"I can assure you," I answered, "that I am not an angel."

Ed Westlake was the next to enter the interrogation. "What was the year of your birth?"

If I had told him 1939, it would have opened a snake den for sure. If I had said 1839 then I would have been ten or eleven when I traveled with Sheb. If I had said 1739 that would have put me close to one hundred, fifty years. "Sir, to be honest I cannot answer that question."

I'm sure I had not satisfied their curiosity, but I'm also sure I would be faced with the quest later on. I was not free of such inquiries.

I was able to acquire the horses and equipment that the highway men had had. So my mode of travel would be similar to years past. I saw time advancing too fast and I longed for a time when crossing a river I had run across a curious but friendly tribe of Indians there were roads and trails over Shasta and the Siskiyous. I once again would go near the place on the river that has caused such questioning. I would once again see if there were scars of a lost civilization. This time I would be alone in case of an unwanted reaction. Lost civilizations were in the past, not in the future to be regained. I have only recorded the highlights of the inquiry. Some things were mysteries in my own mind. The question had been raised again about medical training. The speed and precision of my knife throw seemed to them other worldly, so I was questioned as if I were an outer space alien. The knife wound in the wrist of the robber was longitudinal at a precise area where no main blood vessels or tendons were damaged.

I was lonely and somewhat depressed with questions I could not, or would not, answer. Desert Flower was never to be again. The friendship and companionship I had had with Sheb would not be transferred over to his son, Ken. I wanted to go home, but where was home. I was sure that the cove in the canyons would no longer be mine.

CHAPTER ELEVEN

In the other time I had been somewhat involved in a mining town called Ashwood which was twenty-nine miles east of Madras. A railroad had been built from The Dalles to the little town of Shaniko. Shaniko had become quite the bustling hub-bub, because it was there that the farmers would bring their sheep and wheat to be shipped on the railroad that ran both east and west from The Dalles. From Shaniko there was a stage road that ran south through the town of Antelope and onto the town of Ashwood. Between the mining town of Ashwood and the later established town of Madras there was a very large successful ranch. In the other time it had been a cattle ranch and I had worked there as a young teenager. The ranch had been a very impressive part of my young life so perhaps I need to go there to secure my life again. In the time I found myself in, I was sure it dealt more with sheep.

Prineville, probably the oldest established town in this area, had been mostly cattle country and I had known of many battles between the cattlemen and sheepmen mostly because a lot of sheepmen would allow their sheep to graze land that was claimed by the cowboys. Groups of the cowboys would then go about shooting sheep. The ranch on Hay Creek had enough holdings that this problem, though minimal, still overflowed often enough.

My being a man had been identified on that ranch. It had even involved my first love and first experience of loss due to death. Maybe, just maybe, I could find fulfillment again at Hay Creek.

I suppose for the next six years I found, if not fulfillment, I did find solitude. I was given a mule-drawn wagon that served as living quarters. Each springtime would be sheep shearing and each fall a large drive to Shaniko which was about thirty-five miles. The rest of the time I would be tending sheep.

I had been almost successful in forgetting my quest for a reason for my being and the mysteries of existence in a foggy state of mind. I said almost. It was sheep shearing time again on the ranch and they hired several immigrants from Mexico to help in a fast-paced procedure. One morning as I walked into the shearing barn, a middle-aged Mexican man looked at me with shock written all over his face. "Ay chihuahua! Mama mia! Ah, señor, this can't be, ay chihuahua!" The foreman quickly came to me to ask what I had done to upset the Mexican man."

"Sir, I have no idea. I've never seen him before."

The Mexican man apologized, bowing several times and said. "I work now."

Late that evening the Mexican man came to my wagon and asked if he could talk with me explaining his reaction. "I was hoping you would," I answered.

"My family heritage was from a small tribe of Indians in what is now Central Mexico. They had almost been wiped out by another tribe along with the Spaniards. All that was left was one man and his daughter. The man had been badly wounded when a white man found them. He had been robbed of all possessions and had traveled many days with minimal water or food. The man and his daughter had a shelter with provisions and water so nourished the white man. In return the white man must have been a medicine man because he operated on the Indian man (my heritage) and reset a broken leg bone."

"The white man and the daughter fell in love and she bore him a son and then she got a deadly disease. Just before she died, the white man, broken hearted, left and said he must go to Oregon. Now, Sir, at that time there was no such place as Oregon. The Indian man supplied him with horses and riding gear. He was also an artist and drew a portrait of the man that has been passed down through many generations with this story. I'm first in my family to have the privilege of coming to the mysterious country, Oregon, and I have carried the picture with me."

With that, he gently unwrapped a very old painting. My mind rushed back to seeing loving, but tearful eyes bidding me goodbye. My old saddle came to mind again, with the inscription, "Mi Amigo" and underneath "Mi Amore." I sat there for some time with my eyes closed, shocked, and trying to gain victory over my own emotion.

Juan, the Mexican man, finally touched my shoulder. "Are you alright, Sir? It seems to me that you are familiar with this story, but it is too mysterious for me."

"Yes, Juan, there is much mystery involved, but please take your picture home and never mention me again."

"Sir, you must be the same man, then, but how is that possible. Do hundreds of years not affect you? Who are you?"

Two men were missing from the shearing barns the next day, nor could they be found on the ranch.

I must visit the cove once again. Now there was a road to the bottom of the canyon and a house with a thriving orchard. The family that ran the orchard were the McKaferty's. Mr. McKaferty was away at another ranch of his in Prineville, but his wife was friendly.

"Ma'am. I really don't expect you to believe the story I'm about to tell you, but that may be immaterial to my request. You see, ma'am, I lived in the canyon for some time, years back. I buried my wife and some belongings on that rise over there and I must see if I can find them again."

"Clark Redham was the first person, other than the Indians, to take up residence here. We bought the cove from him. You can dig on that rise if you want to, but if it is indeed an ancient Indian burial ground you might have trouble with the Indians themselves."

"Ma'am, I will not disturb the grave of my wife. I only want to find some of my belongings." I had buried the old saddle and the opal necklace wrapped in several layers taken from Desert Flower's teepee. I was just unwrapping the old saddle and opal necklace when Mr. Mckaferty walked up the hill.

I held the necklace high in the air and called out to Wanken Tonka in the Sioux dialect.

"The woman is no longer mine. The children are no longer mine. The horses are no longer mine, the land is no longer mine. I am alone. I will remain alone until the stars no longer shine." I bowed my head and through the whispering winds I heard Desert Flower say, "You'll never be alone. I'm with you always." I was weeping profusely as I placed the opal necklace over my head and packed the old saddle on my packhorse and rode to Ashwood. There I bought a small house so I could store my few belongings and have a place to lay my head when necessary. After this is when I went to The Dalles and hired on at the Oregon Trunk Railroad Company. Two railroads were in a wild and embattled race to put a rail between The Dalles and Bend. I had taken the stage out of Ashwood toward Antelope. Out of Ashwood as you left Trout Creek, there was a very narrow canyon road that was barely wide enough for the stage to travel. Stopping in Antelope we then went another seven miles or so to Shaniko. The rail out of Shaniko to The Dalles would be abandoned when the rail from The Dalles to Bend was put through. Later that rail would connect with the California rail to complete a north-south route. Many new little towns would spring up along this new rail line.

I was hired on as a wagon driver. I would be hauling gravel and fill from point to point. Sometimes I would haul dynamite from the train that followed to the blasting area, Tool sheds and storage areas were set up plus a box car or two that were used as sleeping quarters.

Several railroad companies had merged, but basically it boiled down to two opposing forces racing in a war of completion. One on the east side of the Deschutes River and one on the west. There were times when, of necessity, they came in close contact. There was one time when the two rails were running parallel as they came to a place that must be tunneled. Instead of joining forces and building one tunnel, two were built and the war raged. There had been a cemetery established up on the flatter area to bury the dead and it was growing. Man-caused rock slides and dynamite blasts in the night were common.

I had cut my hair and beard to a compatible length. To try and disguise my identity, but several incidents with my guns and knife, stories began to spread. Several times after particular destructive times I had volunteered my medical skills. I was mostly left alone to do my job. However, stories were beginning to be heard and spread. One worker came from California where tales were told of a mysterious man who never aged and had many amazing abilities. Several of the Indians worked amongst us and told of the legend of one called White Cloud who had the ability of entering and exiting the spirit world at will.

One night while in my presence, several of these men were embellishing on many of these so called legends. One man, seemingly the lead spokesman for the groups, soon turned to me. "You're rather quiet. What's your take on this?"

"There are all kinds of legends of people doing unimaginable things. Santa Clause for one. How about Paul Bunyan for another, or, have you ever heard of John Henry, the steel driving man, and many others?" Some of these are embellished stories of real people that through wild imagination have been taken way out of proportion. Saint Nicholas was a man or good deeds, but he does not live on at the North Pole, who travels by flying reindeer, or sneaks into houses through fiery chimneys to leave his many gifts.

Fantasy can distant a man's mind to believe the impossible. Common sense would tell us differently. I don't believe Paul Bunyan was born so large that ten storks were needed to carry him to his mother. Nor do I believe he had the companion of a blue ox.

The Indian legend of a man who had the ability to go in and out of the spirit world. Really, come now, spare me.

"Yes, I might have some abilities that you don't, but that doesn't, or shouldn't make me so mysterious."

With that I walked down to the river. I'm not sure if I had brought about a remedial to the situation or not, but they did not include me in their mystic conversation anymore. We really didn't have that much time. Hours were long and work was hard.

The opposing line left the Deschutes before we did and went through the place now called South Junction and Gateway to build a trestle over Willow Creek Canyon just west of the town of Madras. That to us was the Hill Line because a man named Hill was the main man. The Trunk Line continued on up the Deschutes to Willow Creek Canyon and came through Madras in 1911. Land rights and easements wars were mostly over. The two rails came together in the rail formed town of Culver and were more together in the last big obstacle, a bridge over the Crooked River Canyon.

I had not wanted to create a scar when I came to abide at the cove, yet here I had been a part of a mighty scar through the canyon. The Trunk had actually won the race, however, the Hill Line eventually bought them out and the old rail bed was abandoned. Even as I write this account the old rail bed, tunnels, cut and fills are still very visible in most places. Towns like Madras, Culver and Redmond were now thriving. A few others like Mecca, down river from Warm Springs, were mostly forgotten. A road grade was carved into the canyons, called the Mecca Grade, so farmers could bring their crops to the rail there. Mecca had become a wild little place in the canyon with saloons, brothels and gambling joints, but when the rail was abandoned it soon disappeared. The Mecca Grade had been an early route to Warm Springs with a pontoon bridge and cable ferry.

After working with the building of the railroads, I had a fairly good nest egg and should have invested in land that would be under irrigation. In a few years land was going for ten to fifteen cents per acre. This, though, would have put me in the limelight and perhaps changed my future, but my existence, I'm sure, was not to change my future or make a name for myself. I knew that times were advancing. There had been successful experiments in flight and automobiles were beginning to appear. I thought of my hang glider that had brought about such Indian legends. I also thought of the crippled boy I had met many years ago, that was totally intrigued with the thought of conquering flight.

These and other thoughts crowded my mind as I took my slow but determined foot journey back to Ashwood and my little stick house I had purchased. There had been a man that had put a claim on a substantial gold find. His health had failed him and he had gone back to California.

There were a couple of quick silver mines, though, that were producing mercury.

The population there was not really interested in their town booming due to a gold rush. Well, my little house was a walking distance south of Ashwood. I had no furniture at that time so I would build what was necessary. My old Mexican saddle was there although in really bad shape. Once again I thought I would hibernate, work on rebuilding my old saddle and maybe, just relax for a while. To the north of me about a mile at a junction of trails was a tavern that seemed rather active with miners and other population. Just across Trout Creek to the east was a store/ post office combination. A little farther on was another corner where the road led out to the mines was a hotel of sorts. I would not need, or use the saloon or the hotel, but maybe the store once in a while. Ashwood still had the end of the trail mining town reputation, but would soon be dying out.

The Shoshone had ruled the area for as long as most could remember and many of them had been in Indian fights to protect their farms and homes.

I did enjoy a few years of, somewhat peaceful solitude at my little house, but soon winds of conflict were swirling in the air and I was soon to leave my little house to never see it again. Oh yes, I would go back to Ashwood many times, for it held a special place in my heart.

CHAPTER TWELVE

There was a vast difference in my travel to San Francisco as when I first traveled there with Shebard. This time it was mostly by train. The reason for my journey was also of a total different purpose. At this time in mention, there was a battle being fought across the ocean known as the First World War I really wasn't sure if I would be considered, but I was going to volunteer my services as a doctor. No, I had not been declared a doctor by any medical institution, nor did I have any degrees. I couldn't even give any references to my knowledge or previous practice. So then, you may ask, why was I going? I only say that perhaps it was another opportunity to fulfill my purpose of being placed in this special extension of life.

In this American continent, questions were becoming more prevalent as to my existence and it unnerved me, to say the least. My not being able to answer point-blank questions.

Talk about questions, I get a barrage of questions upon my telling the presidio commander of my reason for being there to volunteer.

"Sir, I understand your concern, but I ask you to give me a chance to prove my ability. If you would assign me to your dispensary under the watchful eyes of your honored medical staff. I'm sure I could prove myself as quite useful."

So it was that I was there a total of six months before being shipped out, a civilian in military service. On the German front and the trenches the battle was ferocious. This was not bows and arrows. It was not even six guns and knives, but Gatling guns, cannons, and armoured tanks and land mines. I did not carry a gun as my endeavor was medical. My position was in a near front surgery hospital.

One time a German woman was brought in as a wounded prisoner of war. She had taken shrapnel in the abdomen and legs and was bleeding rather profusely. It seemed rather strange to me that a woman had been brought in.

The military police that brought her in said that she had been an anti-war activist that claimed to be an angel. Her name was Augusta and was, though, coherent, was in much pain.

She had been brought in in the evening and I had worked on her most of the night. I learned later that she had associated herself with another woman and man that called themselves The Survivors my mind did a flip again. Was I supposed to be in association with those who called themselves The Survivors? I really didn't think so nor did I want to be.

This woman was to be transported somewhere else and I was never to see her again.

Before she was transferred, I asked that my identity not be revealed to her. They just assumed that my last name being the same, though very common, I didn't want her reputation tied to me in any case.

So many of the wounded were brought in with such a vast array of wounds, several of them I lost, but the margin between lost and survival leaned strong to survival, so I gained a good reputation with greater recognition as a doctor. I had been accepted as a civilian, but now several suggested I be given military officer rank. I did not accept military rank. After the war I could more easily hide as a civilian doctor that just vanished. Maybe I would just become missing in action. The fact that I had been successful in many severe or traumatic surgeries, had created many questions about my medical training. I have mentioned, early in this manuscript that I had medical training in the Army, in the other time, but not to this extent. Several of my abilities and talents from the other time had been transferred and enhanced to better suit me for a very different existence. In this war time I felt rather fulfilled in my endeavor to preserve life. Perhaps in this, I was fulfilling my purpose. My Sand Creek experience still bothered me that I had not been able to do more.

I was soon to be transferred to the African front when, by chance I had treated an aviator that had a broken arm and had suffered a concussion. As soon as he was well enough, he was to transport several aircraft to France. I asked him what make of airplane he was to fly.

"I'm in command of two Jennys and two Spads, but I only have two other aviators."

I had thoroughly enjoyed aviation in the other time, and my hang glider time with the Indians, so the possibility of flying again was very exciting to me, so I volunteered my time again.

"Have you had any Jenny time?" he asked.

"No, but I see no problems"

So now I was to fly to France and then perhaps go on to Africa. Well, Africa was not to be, but I would soon be going back to America to fly mail. I had flown the Jenny to France, then I also had the opportunity of flying a Spad. No, I never flew dogfights, but I did come close to a Foker triplane. I'm not even sure he saw me, but he was out of his own territory. I was later asked of the color of the Foker triplane with the German insignia. I knew it was red. So as it was, I had had the opportunity to have activated the Barron, but I'm glad I didn't. I might have had the advantage because the sun was in his eyes so I don't think he saw me at all.

Remember, my activities were as a civilian volunteer, not as military. The commander was rather upset though, and let me know in no uncertain terms. I was transferred back to a regular hospital in England until the end of the war.

Getting back to the states, it seemed as though several of the aviators were buying Jennys and either barnstorming or flying mail. I had found a Jenny for a little under six hundred dollars. The OX-5 engine left a lot to be desired as it required much maintenance.

I was invited to join a flying circus where they were performing outstanding aerobatic maneuvers. One fellow had acquired a Spad and offered to sell me that, but I still kept the Jenny and flew to Spokane to fly mail which I did through most of the twenties.

I should have warned you, but the next part of this narrative gets really weird, unbelievable and strange. I make no apologies for I'm only narrating my time after experiencing the day of the yellow glow.

My search through the years has been to make sense of the happenings of that day. I make no claims as being a scientist. My life in the other time had a variety of many interests and as I said in the beginning, I might have thought my experience was mine and mine alone, but I had become aware of at least five other survivors. Had my mind caused it all? Had I had a bad accident and been in some sort of coma all this time. When would I wake up? I had wondered if this old world had been in a collision with some other planetary system that had thrown it backwards through a space worm hole, or black hole. I would think that if something that traumatic had happened there surely would be NO survivors, but here I was inherent in life.

Well here goes. I told you this part was getting weird. Now I began to wonder if I really was the same person I had been, or if I was a different personification altogether.

Yes, here goes the big step into weird. I knew the trail of my grandparents had been from Germany to Minnesota, to North Dakota and then to Deer Park, Washington. I knew my grandparents had moved to Deer Park in 1906 and that my grandpa had built and pastored a church there in 1906. Yes, I had met my great-grandmother in North Dakota in about 1877 and had seen my very young grandfather. Now I would go to church in Deer Park and even meet my supposed father. I wanted to see if there might be any family resemblance.

Maybe I was schizophrenic, or had a split personality. If so, how could I get back to normal? My father at this time, 1921, would be twelve years old. Yes, I know you don't have to remind me. Strange. How can this be true? All these things had not been answered for me yet.

Pastor Wilhelm welcomed me and introduced me to his family. He asked me how I had come to know about the church. I told him I had been flying mail out of Spokane and that I lived on Hangman Creek and a man I had met there sang great praise of him holding him in high esteem. The pastor told me that he too had lived on Hangman Creek and that I looked very familiar, but didn't recall ever meeting me. I moved from Hangman Creek to north of Hillyard district which was closer to the airport I was using. In other words I kind of disappeared again.

In my off flying time, I had been doing mechanic work on my airplane and several others at the airport. The Jenny had basically been a trainer so I extended my job by training several others to fly. Many times I would fly over Deer Park and see the little white church and up the hill away to the little farm where a pastor was raising his large family.

I had bought a 1923 closed cab Model-T pickup and built a trailer to haul behind it. So it was that in twenty-nine I sold the Jenny, packed my belongings and was enroute back to Oregon. I had been tempted several times to just go to the pastor and spill the beans of my story. Perhaps it would have broken the spell and I would be transported to another future life again. Yet on the other hand, I might have pushed the situation to the limits and forced myself in a mental facility. The other survivors, that I had gained knowledge of, had forced their way forward trying to protest advancement and had found trouble for themselves without much success. Myself on the other hand, when questions of my own or of others got too complicated, I would go into hiding. Maybe that's my weakness, but here I was again putting along in my Model-T going somewhere else.

Well I ended up back in the Central Oregon area. The Bureau of Reclamation had started building an irrigation canal from the town of Bend. Eventually it would reach the Madras area to irrigate forty-nine to fifty thousand acres. The Opal Prairie and madras had been a high and very dry area, with the Deschutes and Crooked Rivers at the bottom of a thousand foot deep canyon west of Madras. Of course Willow Creek ran through Madras, but mostly dried up in the summertime. All in all Madras had been a harsh place to live. Windy and dry. When the irrigation canal reached there it would bring about drastic change.

So anyway I headed back to the area. Changing my dress and hairstyle might disguise me for a while. The construction of the irrigation canal would be similar work as building the railroad except now they would probably have more fuel powered equipment.

The canal route had to be similar to the railroad as to the problem of elevation. The Trunk Line had followed the Deschutes River to the Willow Creek Canyon. The Hill Line had taken on a steeper but more direct line. The town of bend was a thousand feet higher than the elevation of where the canal would come to just northwest of Madras. The entire route of the canal would be about forty-five miles, so it would have a good flow. In 1930 the North Unit Irrigation Project took over at the crossing of the Crooked River and tunneled through the Saddle Butte area. To follow the canal, road wise, we put in a narrow road over the Saddle at Saddle Butte to the valley on the other side.

I was at this time and place that I hired on as a dump truck driver. The truck was a solid-tired, chain-driven Mack with the radiator behind the engine making up the firewall. I would haul many loads from the Tunnel, up and over the Saddle to fill in gullies and make roads on the other side. The Mack was slow, but low geared enough that it made it over that hill many times.

I had found a little place in the little railroad town of Terrebonne and lived simply.

As I was unloading my few belongings into my house, another man in the little community came over to help. He was also a worker on the canal project whose name was William McKaferty. I really didn't need much help because I really didn't have much. I guess I should be ashamed of myself, for I wasn't very cautious either. As I was carrying some things in, the opal necklace fell to the floor. William quickly picked it up, looking and examining it carefully.

"Where did you get this from?" he asked sternly.

"In the canyon, not far from here is a large spring coming from a bed of pure opal. Sometime ago I went down there and gathered opal to make that necklace to give to a girlfriend I had at the time"

The age of the necklace was rather obvious, but I hoped he didn't notice.

"I know full well where Opal Springs is. My father bought the holdings of the cove in 1889 and I more or less grew up down there. I remember seeing one like this when I was about ten years old. I only then saw it at a distance held in the air by what I figured must have been an albino Indian."

He handed it back to me gently and continued to help me. I had sold my old saddle so I would have space for my few belongings in the Jenny. It had made me sad to do so, but I was glad it was not now in view to bring greater questioning.

In other conversations with William he would often talk of the history of the cove. He told me how his adopted brother had bought the cove from his dad and still lived down there. His main emphasis seemed to try to convince me that no one had ever had residence there before Clark Rodham. Of course there was the big rock down the river away that had the petroglyph, but no one was able to read them. Yes, he agreed that the Indians had been there to fish and hunt, but not to take up residence, as far as he knew.

William McKaferty was a fine gentleman, but the necklace and Indian legend had invaded his mind. He made no reference about the necklace, nor did he openly question my background, so work on the canal went on. I would not run away this time. Legends, mysteries, ghost stories and embellishments would continue. The mind is inquisitive and continuous to search for facts in the unknown and partially known.

Some questions cannot be answered. Common sense will say that some things are only real in our imagination and others can only answer by comparing previously known scientific and archaeological facts. The good book says in one place, "for the invisible thing of him from the creation are clearly seen through the things he has made. Even to his eternal power and Godhead so that they are without excuse." Sometimes in our search we turn to superstition and get all fouled up.

There were also a few that remembered the old railroad day that I ran across at a gathering palace in town. One of those fellows looked at me for some time and then asked, "Did you father or some relative work on the old Trunk Line?"

"My father as far as I know, is still in Washington. To this point I don't believe I have any relatives in Oregon." The man began to rattle on.

"Well, I'll tell you, you sure resemble a guy that was rather amazing as a doctor and as fast gun and most anything he did. I took a bullet in my gut that destroyed my appendix and that guy, sure enough operated on me and within a week or so I was as fit as a fiddle." "You can't be him, but you sure resemble him. I reckon he'd be about seventy or eighty or even ninety by now."

Common sense told both William and this man that I couldn't have been the actual man that they had come in contact with, but of course the necklace brought an elevated curiosity to bear in mind.

Nothing out of the ordinary happened along the canal until December of 1941. We were sure that war was on its way, but December of 1941 confirmed all our fears. Most things were turned to profit the war effort. I had thought of volunteering my service in the medical field again, however my last ten years had been a construction truck driver so I didn't think that would set well with the military.

My flying experience had been eleven years prior with only ragwing single engine rating. I hate to say so, but once again I felt as though my prior experience was being squeezed out by modern technology.

Another thing that I started to notice was in my physical body, from my awakening in the area of my once upon a time home in Bend, Oregon, I had felt a strength and cleanness of mind like never before. Pain and strain had been very minimal all these years. My hearing and sight had been phenomenal, but January 31, 1939 I had woken up feeling a peculiar weakness I could not explain. Upon awakening my eyesight had been blurry for a while.

It took me a while to contemplate the meaning of it all and then I realized that in the other time my birthday had been January 31, 1939. If in the other time it had been this exact date and it was this exact date again, then the other time and this time had collided somehow. If this was the case, would I continue being separated from my real self or would there be a reunion of some kind. I wasn't positively impressed with the thought of a dual personality of sorts. All I could do was go on being who I thought I was. I must go on as abnormally, normal and not fret myself with the oncoming technological and modernistic world that I had once experienced. I have enjoyed my experience and especially my time at the cove with Desert Flower, but that was a long time ago and as is usually the case, time marches on with only memory intact.

There was a trucking company starting up called Bend-Portland that I started with. Airports were being built in most of the towns around the area. Madras and Redmond were both receiving airports that were large and efficient enough for large military aircraft. With both of these airports they were building barracks and personnel type office buildings. There were several lumber mills in the area, but other building materials had to be hauled in. Along with all this there was a concentrated search and gathering of scrap metal of all kinds. In this area it all went to Portland.

I had sold my Model-T pickup and bought a Model-A 1930 tudor. I would try to keep my place in Terrebonne. Although in this situation I would rarely ever be there. Most young to middle-aged men would be in the war. Some middle-aged men with the families had been exempt. Many women went to work in factories and other places that had been thought of as men's work.

I was at first assigned to a federal semi-truck that had a Hercules engine. Later I was transferred to a Peterbuilt that had a two sixty-two Cummins and later on a cabover freightliner with a six seventy-one Detroit diesel.

In that day, the road between Warm Springs to Mt. Hood had not been put in, so it was a lot longer run going through The Dalles. Roads were mostly narrow and curvy and we did not know about freeways. Several times I went south over the Siskiyous, Shasta and through Dunsmuir Canyon. Many times I went through the cut and fill that had changed my relationship with Shebard Douglass, and I would shed tears as my emotions would invade me again.

There really wasn't much of anything during the war years for me that was very newsworthy. My own emotion had to be kept in check, for I haven't wanted to see this advancement in time again. After the war was over I went back to help on the canal project. We finally reached the plains above Madras May 14 of 1946. I had moved into one of the barracks at the airport. There was a huge celebration due to the irrigation and people had come from all over.

I really didn't want to stay around for all of that so I bought a new 1946 Chevrolet pickup. I built a canopy on the bed that would serve as a sleeping place for the next ten years I mostly traveled and saw most of the country.

CHAPTER THIRTEEN

During this time, in Southern California, I heard about a rather small Bible college and decided to enroll. This would be an interesting experience. Several times I would bring up provocative questions just to hear the response. I brought up again, as I did with Ken Douglass and Brent Holdows the question of Genesis one as in adding the word "became" into the statement that the earth was -void and formless. That caused a lot of discussion as to early manuscripts and interpreting of the Greek or Aramaic. The later Hebrew Bible had worded it as "in a beginning."

I also asked, in reference to Jesus ascending up into the clouds, which way is up on a rotating earth? Where is heaven? Maybe it's just in another dimension. Asking questions, in my learning, to find out if I was just in some other dimension. Of course I couldn't tell them of my experience.

I thought it rather strange though, that I graduated from there in 1957. The same year that in my previous time I had graduated from high school. If, in fact, the day of the yellow glow had been in July of 1989, then I had thirty-two years until my reunion with self. Other than working at a sawmill in Northern Idaho for a few years, I now skip to the year of nineteen seventy-nine. That winter had been very severe so I left there and went back to Oregon. This time though I went to the Portland area.

One day I had gone into Gresham to do some shopping when I noticed a well-dressed business man following my every move. I left the store and crossed the street to a hamburger place and he followed me there. When I left that place to go to another establishment, still he followed me, at a distance, yes, but still obvious. I finally turned and walked up to him.

"I'm not aware of who you are, but I have been fully aware of your following me and I'd like to know why."

"I understand that you don't know me personally, however I have known about you, as you have been followed and kept track of for far more years than I have lived. I hope you don't deny having had a conversation with Brent Holdow, a well-known scientist and historian many years ago. Also, with him at that time was a man named Ken Douglass. We have followed a theory since that time. Indian folk lore has been studied back to the early seventeen hundreds."

A Mexican man with a fantastic story and painting had related a story to some of our members. That was over seventy years ago. He was sent to where you were at the time and convinced you were the same man in the very old painting he had.

You have tried to hide yourself many times, but it has not worked.

It is our theory, yes belief that you are a survivor of a far advanced culture that was wiped out by a nuclear cosmic reaction.

"We also see destructive forces advancing in this culture. The atomic bomb has shown us that there is enough destructive force in the hands of man to wipe out the entire world population and now science has been experimenting with all kinds of nuclear destructive weaponry. It is scary indeed and if you, indeed have lived in a far advanced culture, then we could use your advice and knowledge."

He had invited me to sit with him at a table in the hamburger joint. I mostly sat there with my head down and eyes closed. He had presented some facts to me that, no, I could not deny. It was also becoming impossible for me to ignore. In the meantime it angered me to no end.

"If, in fact, your search scientifically has brought you all these facts and figures and you know all the answers then why do you tail me with your hounds as if I could answer your dilemma? Your actions remind me of Romans 1:22 in the Bible professing themselves to be wise, they become fools. I would like to hear your take on this nuclear cosmos reaction, but I again ask, if all of this is indeed factual, how can you expect me to put a stop to your fears? I'm not a scientist. I'm just a plain ordinary man excelling in some things and lacking in most."

"This study of our cosmos and planetary system has many mysteries for sure, but let me start by asking you if you had ever heard of the Chinese discovery, in the sixteenth century called the crab nebula? We believe that the crab at one time had been a planet with a similar atmosphere and distance from its central sun as is the earth globe that we live on, but it exploded into a nebula, or an expanding gaseous mass. We naturally wonder if its destruction came as a result of an atomic nuclear reaction."

Water is made up of two elements, hydrogen which is highly explosive and oxygen which is highly conducive to flame. When separated and then placed back together again they are incompatible and explode turning back into water. We question whether a nuclear reaction could have caused this phenomenon on the crab.

In our search for a lost culture, we can only go back to the year one thousand when two galaxies came into close proximity. The prominent galaxy's sun burned out which would not have prevented its continuous rotation. We have a theory that the smaller galaxy with a larger sun was pulled into the dominant galaxy which would have created a complete renovating action. The burned out sun being replaced by the new sun would have played havoc with the gravitational pull. In the meantime we theorize that a nuclear explosion would have caused a reverse rotation which in theorem would cause a time reversal. We believe that the glow of new sun which was in relatively close proximity would not have left the dominant galaxy in darkness, rather a global warming effect.

In a time reversal, people would not be destroyed but placed in a limbo effect until which time natural rotation caught up with them again.

The survivors, the few in number, would have experienced a mega natural disaster, perhaps being suspended from the earth for some time only partially aware of the disaster. The mental and physical draw would have left them slightly semi-comatose for some time.

"We have been able to contact one other survivor, a woman, who explained a period of approximately five hundred years as semi-comatose, but she had been very argumentative and negative in her reaction and was finally institutionalized."

He again gave me a chance to speak. "I hope you're not planning to institutionalize me, but I cannot answer or solve your problems.

I do believe there is coming a day when this old world will end with the coming of the Lord. Whether he uses nuclear or not, I have no idea, but I really don't think so. Water, well maybe, but not by flood."

Yes, I'll admit I have had many questions about my existence. Questions I cannot answer for you or for me.

I still look at your following me as it were a grade school playground game of some kind. Throughout my life I've tried to help people, mostly on an individual basis. I carry the burden of unsuccessful times and ask what I could have done to alleviate the outcome. Now, Sir, I might appear to you as one that could answer your questions and bring about a workable solution, but I am not. Why don't you take your scientific mind and equations and channel them to a peaceful solution. I believe you're wasting your time pursuing me and elusive theories that have no value.

Now, please let me live the remainder of my life in peaceful privacy. Have a lovely day, sir."

"Excuse me, just one more question. Please how do you explain the Indian legend of giving access in and out of the spirit world?"

"Sir, I built a hang glider. Duh!"

His look of astonishment was priceless.

I moved back over to Prineville and went to work for a place called Clear Pine Moulding. I had worked there about six years when they decided to train me as a forklift driver. I really don't remember much of my first day as a forklift driver, but I do remember waking up in a hospital bed not knowing why I was there. I had asked them several times when they finally told me I had had an accident with my forklift. I kind of remembered the training, but not much more. They then started asking me questions that, again, I felt I couldn't answer.

It shocked me when my wife, from the original time, walked in with one of my daughters. I realized I had been transferred back into my old self from the other time which was now this time. Of course, then the question came to me if my life from, well whatever time it was, was real or not. Even if it wasn't real, I had mostly enjoyed it and could recall every detail.

I went back to a normal (abnormal) life with my wife claiming my mind was nostalgically stuck in the past to the point of being paranoid. I was laid off at Clear Pine and went to work at another little cut stock mill stacking two-by-six inch boards that came to me on a belt out of the planer. I had worked there about two years when one day I got this funny tightness in my chest. I couldn't describe it for I wasn't sure if it was a pressure or if it was that which comes as a premonition of excitement. While the question rolled through my mind as to what the feeling might be, I noticed the sky begin turning to a glassy, but blue haze. The ash of Mt. Saint Helens eruption in 1980 had caused the same kind of overcast so I was sure one of the mountains in the Cascade Range had erupted. The cement beneath my feet began to tremble, just before the yellow came and........

THE END

EPILOGUE

Life, the universe, weather, the seasons, and nature itself has many mysteries. Can we come up with answers for them all? Well, no we can't.

People with great education, solving all kinds of scientific equations, are still limited. Even a guy like me who has had the opportunity to live many years and have had a myriad of experiences cannot save the world from its own insecurity. Should this fact discourage us from doing what we can, when we can? Fear can keep us from succeeding.

I've heard many people state what they believe is fact only to try and excuse themselves at a later date when they were proven wrong.

Alright, you really don't believe I was personally a survivor of a nuclear cosmos reaction. Well, your belief doesn't make it true or false. A man once said to me, "I don't believe in no Hell."

My answer was, "Five seconds after you're there, you'll be a firm believer."

It really doesn't bother me if you do or don't believe my story. Uh, maybe it should, but with the prophecies (no matter how we interpret them) of the Bible, it behooves us to take the more earnest heed. Science, the Bible, and common sense tells me this old world will one day cease to be.

Okay, I believe that I really do. In the meantime I'll live my life, thankful for the opportunity I have been offered doing the best I can however futile it might be.

Douglas E. Wiese

CPSIA information can be obtained
at www.ICGtesting.com
Printed in the USA
LVHW031914180423
744700LV00012B/31

9 781647 498771